A FLOCK OF
BLACKBIRDS

Also by Susan Noble

Before and After the Darkness
Collected Poems
The Dream of Stairs: A Poem Cycle
Drifting Between Empty Tramlines
Inside the Stretch of My Heart

A FLOCK OF
BLACKBIRDS

Selected Short Stories

Susan Noble

AESOP Modern
Oxford

AESOP Modern
An imprint of AESOP Publications
Martin Noble Editorial / AESOP
28 Abberbury Road, Oxford OX4 4ES, UK
www.aesopbooks.com

First paperback edition published by AESOP Publications
Copyright (c) 2014 The Estate of Susan Noble

ISBN: 978-1-910301-05-0

CONTENTS

CONTENTS

Preface

About the book

A Flock of Blackbirds is a selection of short stories and novellas written by my sister, Susan Noble, who died in 1974 at the age of 31. Susan's output of fiction and poetry in the final ten years of her life was prolific and to mark the fortieth anniversary of her death, the stories in this volume are being published in hardback, paperback and Kindle for the first time, along with four volumes of her poetry, *The Dream of Stairs: A Poem Cycle; Inside the Stretch of My Heart*; *Before and After the Darkness*; and *Collected Poems*, as well as her novel, *Drifting Between Empty Tramlines*.

Many of the stories in *A Flock of Blackbirds* are triggered by the quotidian experience of living and working in central London in the late 1960s and early 1970s, yet beneath the fragile surface of her acute observations of domestic and office life in the city, intensely spiritual insights are being played out, sometimes delicately, sometimes shockingly, but always movingly.

Profits from the sales of all six volumes are being donated to three charities: Mind, the Samaritans and Sane. For more details, see page ix. Facsimiles of the original typescripts and manuscripts are available online at:

www.aesopbooks.com/susannoble

Martin Noble
Oxford, 2014

About the author

Brought up in South London, my sister, Susan Noble, was the second of three children. Her childhood was enriched by being part of our large and closely-knit Jewish family. Unfortunately stricken by polio (then known as infantile paralysis) in her early years, Susan went through life with a degree of physical handicap which she was to overcome with courage and determination.

Educated at Croydon High School, Susan studied English at Somerville College, Oxford. After graduating, Susan worked in London, first at the Royal National Institute for the Blind, dictating books for transcription into Braille, and later at the National Central Library in London, where she qualified as a Chartered Librarian.

Susan's exceptional sensitivity was reflected not only in the intense outpouring of poems to be found in *The Dream of Stairs, Inside the Stretch of My Heart*, and *Before and After the Darkness*, but also in the short stories that make up this collection. In these haunting, poignant stories, she chronicles her personal response to the world around her, while vividly portraying the inner landscape of her own mental and emotional struggle.

Judith Frankel
Netanya, 2014

Susan Noble

One's first impression of Susan was of fragility. She was an acutely sensitive person, but her physical and emotional fragility really masked a very great spiritual strength.

Her sensitivity indeed was not directed only towards herself, but towards others. She was sensitive to the needs of others, and her strength and also perhaps some of her inner conflicts came from a deep desire for goodness which could not be matched in reality by the world as she found it.

Susan passionately wished to be independent; she struggled for it from the time she went to university, and throughout her work as a librarian, and she was able to maintain it to the very end.

There was an intellectual and emotional intensity which burned within her and which predominantly found outward expression in her writing and when she expressed herself thus she did so with great imaginative power and also with an uncompromising honesty and integrity.

The late Rabbi Dr David Goldstein
South London, July 1974

Publisher's note

All profits from the sale of this volume are being donated to the following charities:

The National Association for Mental Health
www.mind.org.uk

www.samaritans.org

www.sane.org.uk

A flock of blackbirds
They cry and cry
And turn and turn about the sky
They fall down on the brown fields
Where the farmer's plough
Has turned the worms
And up they fly
Blackbirds
In a crowd
I hear them call
I see them all

The wind is blowing on my window
And a voice seems to come from nowhere.

'A Flock of Blackbirds', from
Inside the Stretch of My Heart

1 Pigeons

MAGGIE SMILED. 'This park is very patriotic.'

They passed yet another bed of blue corn-flowers and red and white carnations. The mingled scent was diffused by the August heat and clung to the gusts of air that swirled around her hands as she walked briskly down the path. She could feel the air, soft and cloying, like warm, melted chocolate. Her feet itched with the heat and her hair pulled at her scalp in hot stabs. She heard a soft crackling, as though it were drying up into a singed frizz, like the shrivelled clumps of undergrowth that were being pruned by the park-keeper.

'Lovely day, girls,' he said, looking up from his clipping and winking his left eye as they passed him. It closed slowly and seemed reluctant to open again, as though drugged by the heat.

'Glorious,' replied Pamela and then giggled as they reached the next path. 'Look at my lovely sunburn and freckles. I simply revel in the heat.'

The skin of her face, always tinged with pink, was now blazing an angry purple. Her hair was tied back into an old-fashioned pony-tail. It was bright ginger, almost orange, reminding Maggie of a painting book she had owned at the age of four, filled in with all the wrong colours.

The two girls were employed as temporary clerks at Gunnersmith & Halters, a shipping company on the

Embankment. The work involved measuring distances on maps with pieces of cotton. It was simple, but finicky. For Maggie, who had two months to spare before starting her secretarial course, it was relaxing; whereas Pamela, who had just failed her final shorthand exams, found it irksome.

In their office, cluttered with maps, documents and cotton, four other clerks were employed at the same task, and since none of them took the work very seriously, the room was littered with magazines, scarves, shopping baskets, biscuit packets, novels and cosmetics. Roy, their supervisor, complained about the mess from time to time but with little success; his irritation at their untidiness had evaporated into weary resignation.

Maggie enjoyed the work. School was behind her and she was compensating for the past discipline of exams and uniforms by revelling in her freedom. Her evenings were spent going out to parties and movies. She had been seeing Tony for just over a year and had been longing to leave school so she could have more money to spend on clothes and make-up.

She was petite and plump, fresh-faced with curly blonde hair, and knew she was just an average person, the type of girl easily catered for by boutiques and women's magazines. She would often meet people who looked like her, and strangers would come up to her and then apologise, having mistaken her for someone else.

Sometimes Pamela would say, 'You're lucky to be so normal,' and Maggie would grin and reply, 'I suppose I am.' She never really thought about it for very long.

Since leaving school she had reacted against too much thinking.

Maggie had devised a philosophy for herself whereby it was good to be happy and to spread this happiness. She was generous and spontaneous, devoid of malice or complexity. But sometimes her normal cheerfulness and levity would be jerked to a halt by a street accident or a song or a quarrel, and then she would stop what she was doing and start to think quickly. Her heart would miss a beat and she would see everything very clearly as though a pink veil in front of her eyes had been ripped in two and everything would suddenly appear grey and dusty.

But these moments were rare, especially when she was with Tony. He would do this sort of thinking for her. As she looked at Pamela's purple skin and orange hair, an unpleasant sensation flickered up her back. For a moment she wished that Tony was with her. He was perpetually buried in thought. His normal expression was one of worry, and whenever she saw him nervously adjust his spectacles, it was as though the weight of worry had been removed from her own mind and taken over by his. His long fingers would twiddle with the corners of his spectacles and then tweak a strand of black hair off his forehead, and the pink veil would descend again.

'I wish I was at home,' said Pamela. 'At least I could get a gulp of fresh air. Apparently it's been raining there all week.'

'Where's home?'

'Durham. A farm. Lots of lovely fields and trees. But

then if I was at home I wouldn't be able to see Roy every day.'

Maggie giggled. 'I didn't realise you felt that way about him.'

'I'm not sure how I feel.'

They walked over to the three beech trees, and Maggie spread out her mackintosh and knelt down on it. Her knees were fat and pink against the black oilskin. She opened a bag of sandwiches and began to eat, while Pamela leaned her head against the tree trunk, shut her eyes and fell into a doze.

As Maggie finished her first sandwich, a pigeon perched itself on her knees. She threw down some crumbs and two more pigeons appeared.

She had suddenly lost her appetite. The pecking birds opened their beaks voraciously. They repelled and yet at the same time intrigued her and she wanted to see more of them.

She crumbled up the remaining three sandwiches, so that bits of egg and breadcrumbs lay scattered over the grass. She sat back on her heels and smiled as the greenness before her became submerged beneath grey and white bodies, twitching and stalking and pecking.

Their breasts were swollen yet bony; their claws were arrogant. They pattered to and fro like toddlers, confident of their mother's affection for them, and Maggie surveyed the bobbing army of birds with pleasure. She had done her good deeds for the day and fed the hungry creatures. Some of them looked quite thin and even the plump ones were not particularly healthy-looking but had feathers missing and claws clogged together with dust.

Pamela snorted slightly in her sleep and opened her mouth for breath. Her eyelids flickered and then opened. She stared blankly at the sea of white birds and then suddenly screwed up her eyes, putting her hands over her ears like a child trying to blot out an unpleasant scene.

'Sorry – did it give you a shock?' said Maggie.

Pamela did not reply. She stayed hunched up against the tree-trunk, her face contorted and her fingers pressed against her head. The purple skin was gradually turning white. Maggie's heart began to thud. She stood up abruptly and shooed the birds away. Some of them still remained waddling around her shoes. She picked up a handful of egg and crumbs and threw it as far away as possible. The rest of the birds quickly moved, as she began to kick out with her feet. She shook Pamela by the arm.

'Open your eyes, Pamela. It's all right. They've gone.'

Pamela opened her eyes tentatively and jumping up, ran across to the path. Maggie ran after her as they made their way back to the entrance of the park. The red, white and blue of the flowers tossed and zigzagged jerkily as they ran.

'I'm sorry,' said Maggie.

'I don't know why I'm afraid of birds,' said Pamela. 'It's stupid.' She had regained her colour, but was shaking slightly.

Maggie smiled. 'Never mind. We'll soon be seeing Roy again.'

'Thank goodness he wasn't around just now. I must have looked so silly. Don't tell anyone, for goodness sake.'

The heat had subsided slightly and they sat down on a bench. The hot wooden slats sucked into their flesh. Maggie took out a magazine, mechanically opened her handbag and produced a bag of toffees, handing one to Pamela. She opened the magazine and found the dress pattern she was looking for, styled for the average figure. She sucked cheerfully at the toffee, while Pamela took out her paperback and started to read.

They sat for several minutes in peaceful silence. In the background they could hear the distant hum of conversation. The sun was now pleasantly warm and not too hot, but the heat seemed to throb against Maggie's ears in waves. She shut her eyes and thought of the sea. The long, slow waves hurling against the sand and then flicking back, curling up underneath ...

She remembered her last holiday in the South of France. She had spent most of the time sunbathing and Tony had done a lot of reading. Behind the blackness of her eyelids she visualised his face, white and thin, with gleaming brown eyes. His features always seemed to be moving slightly, she reflected. That was because he did a lot of thinking. It seemed a pity somehow. She just liked to laugh and be happy.

There was a slow, scrunching noise as a man's footsteps approached.

'Hello, girls.'

Maggie opened her eyes, slowly in the heat, just as the park-keeper had done before when he had winked. Her eyes travelled up the white raincoat to the brown shirt-collar.

'Hello.' She smiled at Roy, rousing herself: she must be friendly to him and help Pamela. She moved to the edge of the seat and smiled again.

'Do have a seat, sir.'

He sat down and looked to either side of him, smirking slightly as he noticed the open magazine that lay creased in Maggie's hands. He turned away and looked over Pamela's shoulder.

'Sartre,' he said and smiled. He opened his briefcase and produced an identical paperback. 'I'm an addict of the secondhand bookshop too, you know.'

Maggie grinned to herself. He was so corny. She could not understand why Pamela liked him that much.

'I wish I had more time for reading,' he continued, 'but everything is such a rush. Of course, once we get this map-analysis over, our workload will get back to normal. We're very grateful for all the hard work you girls have put in.'

He turned round momentarily and gave Maggie a friendly pat on the knee. She pulled a face as he turned back to Pamela again. Still, everybody saw different things in people. She began to think rapidly, as she surveyed his bearded head from the back. Perhaps there was more to him than she could see. Perhaps people were very complicated and only certain people could understand certain other people. The thought was somehow disquieting to her.

The pink veil descended again. She sniffed, He *was* corny. Pamela just admired him because of his beard. She was really very naïve. It was a pity.

She thought about Pamela for a moment and a stab of pain seized her. She really had looked scared when she had awoken to the sight of the birds. Roy opened a bag of sandwiches, took one out and began to munch. Then he threw some crumbs deliberately onto the ground.

A bird appeared, then two, then three. Maggie's heart began to beat quickly again. She looked at Pamela, who was beginning to turn white.

'Roy,' said Maggie, 'there's Mr Glass. He's waving to you.'

'Where?'

'There.'

Maggie stood up and pulled Roy up from the bench. She pushed him towards the entrance of the park. 'He's over there.'

Roy straightened himself stiffly, recoiling from her hands. He looked at her with distaste and walked towards the gate.

Maggie ran back to Pamela. 'Don't panic,' she said. 'I've got rid of him.'

'It's no use,' said Pamela. 'Look – he's coming back.'

Pamela looked up and could see Roy angrily walking back towards them.

'Is this some sort of joke?' he said.

'No,' said Maggie.

His lips were very thin.

'Which college is it you're going to?'

'North London.'

He picked up her magazine and stared deliberately at the dress pattern. A piece of toffee was stuck to it, pressed to the page by the cellophane wrapper.

'I'm not surprised you act in such a stupid, school-girlish way if all you read is this kind of mush.'

He read out the heading: '"Have a good time at the party tonight." Don't you ever do anything intelligent? Don't you ever think?'

Maggie stared at him. She stopped chewing the toffee and found it difficult to breathe. Her heart began to beat quickly and she thought she was going to choke on the sweet. He was looking so angry and she suddenly felt frightened. She could tell by his face that he was about to be extremely rude to her and she wished Tony was there.

'I suppose I shouldn't say this,' said Roy, 'but there are too many silly little girls like you these days for my liking. Why don't you do something with your time instead of eating toffees and playing practical jokes?'

Maggie stared at him stupidly. She kept trying to swallow the toffee, but it wouldn't go down.

'It wasn't a joke,' she said. She felt as though not one but two veils had been ripped from her vision. Everything seemed completely stark and grey. The birds, pecking at the crumbs by her foot, were pale and grey. She tried to close the veil. To joke. To enjoy her toffee. To smile. But she could not.

Pamela sat gripping the bench, her feet pressed tightly together.

'I think you'd better find another temporary job

somewhere else,' Roy said, and walked away.

Pamela stared at Maggie. 'I'm sorry.'

'It's all right.'

The two girls could see Roy's white raincoat retreating into the distance.

'He was horrible to you,' said Pamela. 'I don't like him at all any more.'

'Let's move,' said Maggie, looking at the crowd of birds that had congregated around their feet.

'Don't bother. I couldn't care less about the silly creatures. It's bad luck that you've lost your job.'

'Never mind,' said Maggie. She opened her bag of toffees and turned over the pages of her magazine. She began to read again, chewing slowly.

She felt curiously pleased that Pamela had overcome her fear of birds. She shut her eyes and tried to visualise the beach in France again, but this time she could not even conjure up the sound of the waves, or the contours of Tony's face.

She turned to Pamela. 'Tony will be surprised when I tell him I've lost my job.' She tried to laugh breezily. 'I've never had the boot before.'

It was as though the pink veil had been torn out for good. She looked at the flowerbeds. The flowers, red and white and blue, seemed to hurt her eyes. Each petal moved slightly in the breeze. Her heart beat quickly and she suddenly felt much older.

2   The Visit

AS PENNY CLIMBED the last step to the front door of Jules's house, the memories came flooding back. Between the ages of six and ten she used to visit this house every Saturday with her father, when he was writing regular features for *Pearl*, but she had not seen the editor of that magazine for fifteen years.

She wondered whether Jules would have changed. The front door seemed to have shrunk. Out of habit she peeped through the letterbox and could glimpse the familiar row of oil paintings in the hall.

The letterbox shutter snapped down with a metallic ping and the door opened angrily.

'Go away. I'm sick of all this rubbish,' came the familiar Czech accent. Penny drew back in surprise and Jules peered at her vaguely.

'Oh, I'm so sorry. I thought it was one of those local schoolboys messing about at the door. Can I help you?'

'Yes, I've come from Renshaws Publishers to collect your latest proofs. There's been some confusion, I gather.'

He nodded. 'There has indeed. Come in.'

He shuffled into the lounge in his carpet slippers, stooping heavily. He was still a tall man, but his black hair had now faded to salt, pepper and grey, and he wore thick spectacles. Only his eyes remained the same: large, black and anxious. Even as a child she had noticed those worried flickering eyes darting to and fro. It was a curious nervousness, which contrasted with the expansiveness of his voice. He rummaged in his desk drawer, dropping books and papers.

'I'm so untidy. Please excuse me. My wife is always complaining about it.'

Penny smiled. She could recall Lina's complaining tone. And then the image of her face flashed through her mind, a small head set upon a delicate neck. Her skin was a translucent white, so you could almost see through her, and her deep grey eyes were perfectly shaped. It was an unusually simple face, but it had hovered in her mind over the years as a sort of guardian spirit. Lina used to tease her and scold her as a six-year-old, and Penny giggled as she remembered her own naughtiness.

She looked up and saw Lina's portrait hanging on the wall in front of the piano. It was a large close-up of her face and neck, with the frills of a blue silk collar showing. The forehead was high and pointed like a white egg, and the hair was very black.

There was a shuffling noise as Jules walked towards her, the heels of his slippers flapping against the carpet. The slippers were threadbare and the heels were almost detached from the main fabric.

'Careful,' she said. 'You look as though you're going to trip over your slippers.'

He turned his toes inwards and smiled. 'People always think that, but I know how to manage them. It's the same with editing *Pearl*. Some of my contributors are very temperamental, but I can control them. It's a question of balance.'

Penny laughed. She was determined not to reveal her identity. She wanted to see the real Jules, not the façade he might display for the daughter of an old friend. He sat down on the sofa and handed her a pile of folders.

'The material's all here. I would have brought it round to the office myself, but my back's been very bad and the best way to alleviate the pain is either by lying down on the sofa or by playing the piano.'

Penny looked surprised.

'You don't believe me? Watch.' He shuffled over to the piano stool and sat down on it firmly. 'Note the positions of the arms.' He began to play a few scales and then a series of arpeggios.

Penny wondered for a moment whether he had in fact recognised her, for he had always put on this performance when she was a child. As the arpeggios turned into a waltz, Penny looked surreptitiously at her watch: it was 3.30. The piano-playing was atrocious – the two hands were completely unsynchronised and he kept slipping into the minor key by mistake.

'Jules!' screamed a high-pitched vibrato voice from upstairs and there was a banging on the ceiling. 'Be quiet! That's a horrible row!'

As he continued to play, noisy footsteps came clattering down the stairs. The door opened and a woman stood with her back to Penny in front of the piano.

Penny couldn't help herself. 'Lina!' she shouted in delight.

Lina turned round slowly and Penny gasped. Lina's face was distorted and twisted, mottled with squares of bright red and bright orange like a patchwork quilt, and there were brown scars on her forehead.

'Do we know each other?' Lina asked.

Penny stared at her and tried to smile. 'Yes, I'm Penny Dalton. I used to come here with my father, Thomas Dalton.'

Jules rushed over to her and shook her hand. 'This is marvellous. Why didn't you tell me before?'

'I don't know. It was really Lina I wanted to see again, and I just wanted everything to be natural, the way it always used to be.'

'But it is. We're all the same. Everything's the same. Here am I, playing the piano and there's Lina. It's wonderful.'

Penny stared at him blankly. Perhaps the light had played a trick on her. She looked up again and involuntarily winced.

Lina put a finger up to her cheek and stared at her coldly.

'This is a real surprise,' repeated Jules.

'Yes,' Penny tried to smile.

'No. Penny's changed,' said Lina. 'She's different.'

'She's older, that's all,' said Jules.

'No, it's more than that. She's different as well as being older. There's a different person inside her. You were a very sweet child, Penny, and now you're grown up and sophisticated.'

'Rubbish.' Jules thumped his hand on his knee. 'All young people today are sophisticated.'

Penny giggled, involuntarily.

'She's mocking us, Jules,' said Lina.

'I'm not. Truly I'm not.' Penny wanted to cry. She realised that her face had expressed deep pity for them, before she had time to hide it. She wished she had not come back. The memories of her childhood, which had been tucked away in a neat corner of her mind, would never be the same.

'It's so nice to see you again. I'm working for Renshaws, you see, and I had to collect Uncle Jules's proofs.'

Lina smiled as Penny said the words 'Uncle Jules' and her face softened. 'Well, it's nice to see you, dear.'

Jules sighed. 'One thing I must tell you. *Pearl* isn't as popular as it used to be. Perhaps you have some young friends who write, so you must tell them all about it. We don't get enough support.'

'And Jules runs it all himself. He works so hard.'

Penny suddenly felt as though they were clinging to her.

Jules stood up. 'So come again, and tell all your friends about us.'

'I will,' said Penny.

She walked by his side to the front door, while Lina sat down to play the piano. 'Uncle Jules, what happened to Lina?'

'Nothing. What do you mean? Nothing. Doesn't she play beautifully – like the sound of bells.'

Penny stared at him, open-mouthed. His face was serene and smiling.

'So beautiful,' he said. He patted her on the shoulder, just as he had when she was a child. 'You will come back, won't you?'

'Yes, I will. Goodbye.'

She walked down the steps and into the wide streets. She realised now just how dark and gloomy the interior of the house had been. Outside, the sky was white and empty. She felt numb. She had trespassed upon the past and Lina had seen through her.

As she walked into the market, she saw two girls walking out of a boutique. They were twins and both wore their hair tied back. Their white foreheads gleamed in the sunlight against their black hair.

A pigeon suddenly flew overhead and splashed one of the girls. She laughed as she dabbed her face with a handkerchief.

'Nothing's sacred.'

Penny walked through the market, treading on pieces of tissue paper and silver foil. It started to rain and the water poured down her cheeks. She hurried down the street, wrapping her jacket around her more tightly, and she knew that she would never visit Jules and Lena again.

3   The Train Journey

Rita

THEY SAT in the corner of the compartment, staring out of the window.

'It seems such a waste,' said Rita. She looked across the compartment at her brother Tom.

'Are you against all marriages or simply suburban marriages?'

'Both.'

They stared out of the window. Trees and telegraph poles flashed by. The two women at the other end of the compartment munched ginger biscuits,.

'I'm not against suburbia,' said Rita. 'I just wished Tina wasn't getting married to him, of all people, and to think that she'll spend the rest of her life buried in that little spot.'

Rita had lost all sense of time and place, as she stared out of the windows. The rapid speed of the train precluded any fixed idea of geographical limits. The train as a mobile entity seemed at that moment more real than either London or Leeds, the end-points of its journey.

'It wouldn't matter if he had a bit of initiative,' said Tom, 'but he's just a vegetable.'

Vegetative matter no longer seemed of importance as they swept along the railway line. Rita felt dizzy as a blinding flash of white sky hit her eyes. Blinding white. It sickened her. The sky was cold; cold and empty. They were no longer children. They had grown up. Tina, their sister, was getting married and the flexibility of their parallel living as siblings was now dislocated.

Tom and Rita had little in common: totally different in temperament and lifestyles, they shared one thing: a respect for Tina, their elder sister. Rows of brick houses flashed by – backyards and washing-lines, symbols of the little units that made up the industrial North.

Tom opened a paperback and began to read. Rita forced herself to contemplate the view, to endure the reality of the situation. This was the basic difference between herself and her brother. He would escape into the world of fantasy and the intellect, and she would stare with open eyes at the world outside. To endure, to accept, was her philosophy. She could sense every grain of colour outside the compartment and every flicker of motion within.

The air was damp, the seats were hard, the two women in the corner giggled and crunched, and Tom was lost in his book. She alone surveyed the ugliness outside that was to become the daily background to Tina's life. Why was her sister so selfless, so self-sacrificing? Why did she have to marry George?

She felt a sense of opportunity, as though at this particular moment, halfway through their journey, she could change the situation. It was as though by willing enough, she could halt the wedding. She gazed so intently at the brown fences and grey concrete outside that her vision became blurred. She was utterly alone at that moment, and she had the sense of the complete aloneness of every individual.

The idea of a wedding was a mere pretence, a farce. How could Tina and George be united? How could anyone be joined to anyone else, when everyone's consciousness was so totally different?

There was a rustling in the corner and the woman on the left coughed over her biscuit and said, 'What time does the service start? I must look at my invitation.'

'Two o'clock,' replied her companion.

Rita turned round and blushed as she saw them scrutinising her sister's wedding invitation. Should she and Tom introduce themselves? After their previous remarks it would be too embarrassing, yet something impelled her to speak.

'I think we're going to the same wedding,' she said.

There was a sudden sound of quicker munching and then an odd silence as they gulped down the last crumbs of their biscuits.

'Oh really?' said the woman. 'My nephew George Robson's getting married in Leeds.'

Tom slowly looked up from his book, his face registering acute embarrassment. 'How fantastic,' he said. 'So are we. What a pleasant surprise.'

Rita forced a smile. The woman laughed and passed the packet of biscuits to her.

'Have one of these, love,' she said, and Rita knew that she had been forgiven.

Ruth

I N THE next compartment, Ruth sank into a warm stupor as she sat in the corner of the train travelling from London to Leeds. She stretched out her legs and crossed one ankle over the other. She felt peaceful and vacant. It was a luxury to lay aside the streams of thoughts that normally crisscrossed through her mind like a meshwork of telegraph wires. tempting her to leap from one theme to another.

Now her mind was empty and serene like an endless sheet of black velvet that drew her into the vacuum of an abyss. As she dozed, the black velvet began to form into an image.

The only colourful item of her wedding outfit was a large pink hat with tiny glass cherries sewn onto the brim. She contemplated the event of the afternoon. The wedding would commence at 1 pm and she visualised Tina standing under the *chuppah* – the wedding canopy in the old synagogue; the mournful music of the cantor, swelling to exultation and then subsiding again into tones of melancholy.

On one side of the synagogue stood the men – family and friends, swaying up and down like clockwork toys as they chanted, their bodies bending at different angles and in different rhythms.

On the other side, the women stood, equally mobile, heads turning as they whispered comments of appreciation and, of course, swapped gossip. The younger women and girls would sit more quietly, their heads turned uncomfortably to the far left of the synagogue where the wedding group stood beneath the *chuppah*.

The silk of the rabbi's prayer-shawl shone yellow beneath the lights. The ancient liturgical music resounded in Ruth's ears and she opened her eyes to see a row of backyards and washing-lines bobbing up and down through the windows.

Marsha, the American girl sitting opposite her, yawned slowly. 'Dreary scenery, isn't it.'

'Fabulous,' Ruth replied absently, only half hearing.

'Sad. Look at it. Little families. Scraps of people closeted together in horrible little units. It makes me feel quite ill.'

As she said the word 'ill' she lifted her arms behind her head and folded her hands on top of it. Her black dress hung on her in elegant folds, the neck and sleeves trimmed with a band of green flowers. She lifted her hands off her head, fiddling with some pins in her hair for several minutes and then pulled out two books from her bag.

'I want to read and read and read.'

'Go ahead,' laughed Ruth.

'No, I don't mean now. I mean all my life. Oh God, how can Tina bear to be tied down?'

'She'll adore it, Marsha.'

'Maybe. I don't know…'

Marsha crossed her legs and, pulling out the bookmark, started to read.

Ruth looked across at her surreptitiously. Her thin bones and white skin were perfect, and yet completely cold. Not a trace of expression passed over her face as she read. Her limbs were completely immobile. Yet she could be warm and generous.

They had all three studied at university together and Ruth had always admired Marsha's independence and Tina's domesticity, particularly because she possessed neither of these qualities. She agreed with Marsha that she did not want to be tied down, but without those bonds she felt frighteningly adrift. Days came and passed like pages riffling in the wind.

The man next to her pulled a large book out of his brief-case. Ruth looked across to see the title: *Suburban Family Life in England*. He opened it at the beginning and began to read, fingering his beard thoughtfully and pulling at the hairs in the middle. Suddenly sensing that he was being watched, he looked across at Ruth and raised his eyebrows with mock amusement.

'Are you also interested in the problems of suburbia?'

'I suppose so.'

He smiled gently and perceiving that Ruth had no wish to expand on this statement, shifted his position and continued to read.

Ruth gazed through the train window at the telegraph wires as they wove together and parted and in her mind she was back at her parents' home…

'When did you tell Gordon you were breaking it off?' asked Margaret.

Ruth glanced away from her mother. 'Yesterday. I don't particularly want to discuss it. I'm just letting you know.'

'There's no need to be rude. You're looking very pale. Have you been taking your iron supplements?'

'Yes.'

'I think you're foolish about Gordon. I can't believe it. It was all settled in my mind. I'll have to write to all the family. I don't know what they'll think.'

Margaret picked up the teacloth and began to wipe the stainless-steel blades of a pile of knives. Damp smears lingered on the steel and she rubbed more vigorously.

'Nobody's perfect. The trouble with you is you expect perfection in everyone. Gordon may not be brilliant, but he's a man you can respect.'

Ruth sighed. 'It's too complicated to explain. I didn't expect you to understand.'

'I don't choose to understand your motives, Ruth because I'm your mother and I happen to care about your future.'

The two women stood across the kitchen table confronting one another. Their faces were similar, pale and large boned, except that Margaret's hair was knotted up in a bun, and Ruth noted that it was almost grey. Her mother's features were severe and classical, and Ruth sensed for the umpteenth time, that Margaret was disappointed in her.

As she stood opposite her, she was conscious that her own features were a poor imitation of her mother's. It was difficult to detect why. A hint of irregularity or bluntness. The effect was far removed from the beauty that Margaret Shaw had possessed in her youth.

'Mother,' she began. She wanted sympathy.

'You're a fool, Ruth. I'm sorry, but I must be frank.'

'Oh, bloody hell.' Ruth slammed the kitchen door closed behind her, left the house and ran down the road.

She was exhausted yet she knew she had to get back to her bedsitter. The shops and offices on either side of the road swerved and lurched. She felt giddy, hot and then cold. She was too tired to go back by public transport so she waited for a taxi at the corner of the high street.

As she waited, she could feel the crowds jostle past her on the pavements. She could sense their energy and she simply wanted to sleep. She felt faint and her body started to sway when she saw in the distance the orange light of a taxi. Half an hour later she opened the front door of the house where she rented a room.

'Good evening, Miss Shaw,' a voice came from the hall. It was Mr Schwarzbart, her landlord.

'Good evening.'

'I have something to tell you.'

He beckoned her into his kitchen at the end of the hall. She sat down on the rocking chair in the corner. Mrs Schwarzbart, the landlord's wife, a buxom, blonde *hausfrau*, was chopping vegetables in the corner.

Ruth leant back against the chair and rocked, listening to the comforting chopping sound of her vegetable knife.

'My wife and I have decided to move to Brighton. I am retiring, you see.' He smiled courteously, thin upper lip over large white teeth. 'You understand. We are so sorry to cause all our delightful tenants this inconvenience, but you do understand...'

'Of course.'

'So in a few months you will need to find somewhere else to live. I have just been telling Moira and Janet on the ground floor.'

'Of course.'

Her eyelids began to twitch. She simply wanted to sleep, to sink into nothingness. She focused her attention on the chopping.

'You have been a very good tenant, Miss Shaw.'

'Oh yes, very good, very good,' his wife echoed, looking round, a yellow plait of hair gleaming on top of her head. She wiped her fingers against her hips. Ruth lowered herself out of the chair.

'Thank you, Mr Schwarzbart. Please excuse me. I'm very tired—'

'Anyway, you won't need furnished lodgings for very long now.' He laughed and winked knowingly.

'You mustn't work too hard, Miss Shaw,' said Mrs Schwarzbart, her voice sounding strident against the silence of the entrance hall. 'Especially you.'

She reached her room and collapsed onto the bed. Always the reminder of her illness.

She stretched out her hand, mechanically took a pill from the capsule on the bedside table. It lodged uncomfortably in her gullet as she lay stretched out on the bed. She was too tired to move.

She shut her eyes. A black screen. Her mother's pale face, grey bun, waving to and fro, admonishing her: *You're a fool, Ruth.* And then she saw Gordon, the thin, mousy hair, and owl-like spectacles; always kind, always sincere – she did love him. Even now she knew that, but she did not want to marry him.

It had taken her a long time to realise just how strongly she didn't want to marry him. Only a week before the engagement party. It was cruel to Gordon, unfair to him, possibly imprudent to herself. Yet she had made her decision. The figures faded out of her inner vision and she could only see blackness. The dark, a sinking, a yawning … and then she slept.

Ruth awoke at 5.30 in the morning. The dawn sunlight gleamed in through the greenness of the trees above. An ecstasy of birdsong and pinpoints of yellow sunlight. She opened the windows and could see soft, golden particles in a long ray of sunlight that slanted onto her bedside table.

She lifted her hand and chopped the ray in two. She lowered her hand and the yellow light joined up again. It was a childish thing to do.

If only she could be independent, not need anyone or rely on anyone. She felt as though she were living in a vacuum and she wanted to break through, like piercing flesh with a knife-point.

She wanted to confide in someone, to talk and talk, boringly, ramblingly, at devastating length. She laughed as she flicked through her address book. Who could she inflict it on? Not Tina, who was too wrapped up in her forthcoming marriage; not Marsha, who considered such relationships a complete waste of time anyway.

Her cousin Rob was the ideal person, but he was in Israel, working on a kibbutz. Harriet, her former flatmate, would be consoling without understanding. She discarded name after name mercilessly and sighed. It was appalling to know so many people so superficially.

She whistled a Viennese waltz to herself as she began to dress and just as she was pulling a sweater over her head, she thought of Rayah. She pulled it half over and gazed at herself in the mirror.

The pink sleeves dangled awkwardly over her shoulder and her hair was caught up in the polo neck – long black hair. She pulled it out so that the pink wool of her sweater was almost totally submerged and hidden. Long black hair. It made her feel like a plant as it coiled around her shoulders. She slipped her arms into the sleeves and briskly pulled her sweater down.

Rayah was the perfect person to confide in. She hadn't seen her for six months. It had been too embarrassing after Rayah and Nicky had split up. She had felt somehow alienated from Rayah, as if in loyalty to

Nicky. But Rayah spoke so little and understood so much. Ruth looked out of her window again and visualised Rayah dancing in a ring round the trees, just as she always used to when she was living with Nicky.

Rayah was childish, like herself, and did not attempt to hide it. She saw the tiny figure with long red hair and freckled face dancing round and round the tree in blue shirt and blue jeans and bare feet. Rayah always wore blue and Ruth always associated her with the summer. Many people thought Rayah was affected: her nonchalance, her long silences, her poetry. Perhaps these were affectations, Ruth reflected, but they were still part of who Rayah was.

As Ruth stared at the imaginary image of Rayah dancing around the trees, she suddenly felt jealous. Rayah was never alone. She formed links with everyone, like a spider's intricate web and then she deliberately detached these threads and affected a sadness at being alone. At the same moment she realised that telling her problems to Rayah would be like dropping her most intimate, personal diary into the depths of the ocean.

The truth was, there was no-one to whom she could talk about this. She tugged at her hair in irritation as she recalled her mother's look of pity.

Nobody's perfect. Gordon may not be brilliant, but he's a man you can respect.

But that was the trouble. She did not respect Gordon. She smelt again the scent of blackberries he had been eating as he kissed her the week before. She did not want men to smell of blackberries. He had looked like a little boy, the stains of fruit juice on his cheeks and chin, and the expression of concern as she recoiled.

'Are you feeling well, Ruth?'

That was the hold that Gordon had on her, and she had to break it once and for all. She could not live with his pity all her life – or his stupidity. Their final quarrel had been triggered by the concert last Wednesday.

She was waiting for him outside the town hall. He was twenty minutes late. He ran up to her, panting, pushing back his spectacles with one hand and twirling his scarf over his shoulder with the other.

'Sorry I'm late, love. I was held up by a bloody official at the tax office.'

'Yet another bloody official,' she said mockingly.

He stared her straight in the eye, a habit she found intensely irritating.

There's no need to mock me, Ruth.'

'I'm not mocking, but you must admit that you're prone to being plagued by "bloody officials".'

He looked so sure. Gordon had very little sense of humour. Ruth tried to remind herself for the umpteenth time of his better qualities.

He began marching into the concert hall. The heavy slap-slap of his sandals irritated Ruth. She felt herself recoil as he put his arm around her.

'What's the matter with you today?' he said.

'Nothing.'

He continued striding into the hall. Even though he had arrived twenty minutes late, there were still empty seats at the front of the hall and he led the way towards them and sat down in a front seat, near to the centre

41

aisle.

An official immediately walked up. 'These seats are reserved, sir.'

'I'm very sorry, but these tickets say that we can sit in the first ten rows.'

'I know that's what they say, sir, but—'

'Don't argue with me, we have every right to sit here.'

'Oh Gordon, stop it!'

'Just keep out of this, Ruth.'

'Don't be so pompous.'

He turned towards her and his eyes were fixed and glaring angrily behind his spectacles. She stared at his white skin, as white as the skin of a small boy and smelt again the scent of blackberries. The thin, silky locks of his hair fell over his forehead and across his spectacles. He was clean and white and at that moment she hated him.

'I'm afraid I'll have to report you to the manager,' said Gordon. 'Come along, Ruth.'

He strode masterfully out of the hall and began to bang at the door of the manager's office.

'Goodbye, Gordon. I'm leaving.'

He swung round. 'What are you talking about?'

'I've had enough of this. I want to go home.'

'But why?' He stared at her, panic-stricken.

'Because I don't like you any more.'

It was cruel, but it was the truth.

He stared at her solemnly. 'You're foolish.'

She turned away and ran out of the town hall and down the street. The shop windows flashed by, long panes of glass with her red coat reflected inside each of them. A flash of red against a flash of transparent white.

She looked at the glass as she ran and knew that she was cruel, yet there was nothing she could do about it. It was part of her nature, just as the edge of the glass was sharp. Gordon had intruded upon her in some indelible way. Perhaps it was merely by his love – a normal feeling, yet she resented his intrusion; she resented being loved, and so she retaliated by kicking out at him.

A few days after the town hall concert she was standing in the kitchen, cutting up a loaf of bread; each slice slowly flopped to the drawing board. A heap of crumbs clung to her clothes; she blew them away and began to slice cucumber.

She heard someone walking up the stairs and there was a knock on the door.

'Hello, can I come in?'

'Yes.'

Gordon walked in, his hair wet from the rain and clinging to his head in shiny yellow shades, the lenses of his glasses covered with a thin film of water. He wiped off the moisture with his sleeves.

'I'm sorry about Wednesday night.'

She did not reply. She wanted to wrap her arms around him, but she was angry with him.

'I said I'm sorry.'

'I should hope you are. That scene was totally unnecessary.'

'Well, I don't like being ordered about by officials.'

'Oh for God's sake, don't keep on about officials. Whenever we go anywhere, you end up making a scene. It really gets on my nerves.'

'Well, I thought that man had a bloody nerve telling us we couldn't sit in the front row.'

'But Gordon, it was reserved for special guests.'

Gordon thumped his left hand on the table. 'I don't like these distinctions between ordinary guests and so-called "special guests". What was that guy's name anyway?'

'I don't know. He plays the violin in the Franz Schuller ensemble.'

'I thought he was bloody officious.'

'No, he was only doing his job. Look, Gordon, I've had enough of these scenes. Quite frankly, I think we're through. It's just one row after another—'

'You're completely disloyal to me. You always turn against me, whenever I'm up against opposition—'

Ruth took off her engagement ring and placed it in Gordon's hand.

'I'm sorry, Gordon. Truly I am. We'll have to break it off. The reason I don't support you is that I simply don't agree with your opinions.'

'But you never try to understand my opinions. You don't realise how angry these officious morons make me and—'

'*I don't care!*' Ruth shouted. 'Just go away and don't come back.'

Gordon blinked and laughed uneasily. 'What do you—'

'I mean go away. I'm busy.'

She began to butter the bread vigorously. The slices of cucumber sank into the butter, their edges shaved by yellow blobs.

Gordon looked at her for a long time and then shrugged his shoulders and sighed. 'OK.' He walked out of the kitchen, leaving the door wide open and ran noisily down the stairs.

Ruth paused for a minute, her knife suspended in mid-air, and then, after a moment's hesitation, she slammed the door shut and continued to slice the cucumber.

She opened her eyes as the man next to her accidentally kicked her.

'I'm sorry,' he said and then looked at her curiously. 'What have you got against suburbia?'

'I have an aversion to the idea of people becoming mechanical replicas of each other. I suppose it's just a reaction against my own family. The whole system seems so lifeless ... soulless.'

He nodded his head in agreement. 'It probably seems lifeless to you, but speaking as a member of a suburban family, I find all my three children very unusual – and that's true of all my neighbours too.'

Ruth placed her hat on her lap and fingered the cherries. 'I'm just on my way to a wedding with my friend Marsha.' She nodded her head towards the American girl sitting opposite them who was still completely absorbed in her book. 'Our friend Tina's getting married.'

'How very nice.'

'I suppose so. She was always so successful at school. She used to get ninety per cent in every exam and she was just as successful at university – and now she's just getting married to some bloke in Leeds.'

'You don't think she's making the right choice?'

'I think women should have the right to pursue their own paths, without leaning on a man.'

'Yes, I suppose one doesn't need marriage. One can express oneself in so many ways – through music for instance.'

'Yes, I feel really alive when I'm playing the piano. Do you play an instrument?'

'Only in an amateur way. I play the violin in the Franz Schuller ensemble.'

She quickly looked at the bearded face and felt her heart beating with surprise as she realised that she recognised him.

She looked down at her fingers, and felt a moment of triumph that she was independent.

'So you're glad it's not you who's getting married today.'

Ruth hesitated. She thought about Tina, prepared to give up so much for George; she thought about Marsha, who despised any woman who tied herself down to a man and sacrificed her independence; she thought about Rayah, who had seemed so happy with Nicky until she had suddenly, with clinical precision, ended the relationship for no apparent reason, maybe so that she could once more be a free spirit.

And then she remembered Gordon, his little boy

skin, the hurt in his eyes, and that bittersweet smell of blackberries, and she felt a painful rush of tenderness.

'I'm not sure,' she said.

4   The Fountains

'WHO'S THAT BOY with the long arms?'
Kathy snapped out the question between typing the letters. She placed a small pencil between her teeth and began to check the carbon copy for smudges.

'He's called Albert,' replied Paula.

Kathy laughed. 'He's a scream. He reminds me of a Cornish pastie or a jar of Devonshire clotted cream, the way he speaks.'

'I think it's a gorgeous accent. Don't be unkind.'

Paula walked up to the small mirror on the left wall of the office and parted her hair with a comb. It hung down smoothly on either side, like a pair of black silk curtains.

'I do wish my hair would stay in place. I'm very jealous of you,' said Kathy as she started brushing her stiff brown hair vigorously. It crackled.

Footsteps approached the door. Both girls rushed to their desks and replaced their brushes and combs in their top drawers as Albert walked in. They both looked at him and smiled.

'I was wondering ... er ...if you could tell me how the telex works. My message has got stuck. It's most embarrassing.'

'Of course,' said Kathy, springing up out of her chair and accompanying him to the telex room.

Paula walked back over to the mirror and stared at

her reflection. Small black eyes, a tiny noise and mouth, and very pale skin. She looked like a currant bun. It was cruel of Kathy to call Albert a Cornish pastie. Yet working with Kathy, she too was always mocking people. It was probably the boredom of their work which prompted them to caricature all the other people at the office, homing in wherever possible on their eccentricities.

She turned round briskly as Kathy ran back to her desk, her head folded in her arms and heaving with laughter.

'Not only does he talk like an advertisement for a holiday in Torquay,' Kathy snorted, 'but he makes the most obvious remarks. Have you noticed how he repeats just about everything you say, in almost the same words. It's hilarious.'

There was a slow thud of loud footsteps as Albert returned. Kathy gesticulated to Paula.

'Did you find that the telex machine is working properly after all?'

'Yes, I did find that the telex machine is working properly after all.'

Paula stretched out her arms and took a deep breath. 'It's such glorious weather. I think I'll go for a walk in the park in my lunch-hour.'

'Yes. It is lovely weather. I think I'll go for a walk in the park in my lunch-hour as well.'

Kathy couldn't help it – she collapsed in giggles.

'What's funny?' asked Albert.

'Oh, nothing. It's just the spring sunshine. I feel terribly, terribly happy.'

He smiled politely. 'Yes. I feel happy too,' and walked out of the room.

Paula sighed. 'Oh, Kathy, you are cruel.'

'Never mind. You'll be able to get friendly with *lovah-boy* in the park. High jinks among the rhododendrons.'

'Are they out already?'

'Heavens, I don't know. You'll have to ask Albert for your botanical information. He's sure to be an expert on it.'

They both sighed and returned to their typing.

At one o'clock Paula put on her jacket and walked out of the office into the sunshine. The pavement rang crisply beneath her feet and she trod deliberately over rows of jutting shadows. Black outlines of lamp-posts, tree-trunks and the filigree outline of leaves. Shop canopies, passing children, a precarious ladder and the delicate outline of a kitten. All these shadows lay strewn across the pavement. She skipped over them and slipped through a hole in the hedge into the park. She made her way through a sequence of circular paths to the fountains in the middle.

She gasped. Normally there were only two large fountains in the centre of the bare patch of concrete, but these had been removed and in their place she could see dozens of tiny glass fountains, all in different colours: jade greens, magentas, ambers. She pulled up a deck-chair in front of a ruby-coloured, hexagon-shaped piece of glass, with a small crescent cut out of one side. She stared at it in fascination, mesmerised by the red glow. She felt as though she were being sucked into a pot of plum jam or a bottle of grenadine. The soft shine of glass reflected against the concrete like drops of blood in the sunlight, which filtered through the trees from above.

She was startled by a tap on her shoulder and looked up to see Albert peering down at her.

'Oh hello,' she smiled expansively.

He pulled up a deckchair.

'Aren't these fountains beautiful,' she said.

'Yes, these fountains are beautiful, aren't they.'

She suddenly felt very irritated and wished Kathy were there to share her irritation. Then she looked at him. He was very tall and thin and he did have incredibly long arms. He reminded her of a spindly puppet, which had been her favourite toy between the ages of four and seven.

He slipped a long hand into the pocket of his raincoat and produced a packet of biscuits. A letter fluttered out at the same time. It was caught up by a breeze and whisked away scratchily along the ground. He sprang up and ran after it, but it disappeared under a hedge.

Paula stood up. She could hear some small boys giggling behind the hedge, then saw that they had picked up the letter and were beginning to tear it to shreds. Paula looked up at Albert, who seemed incredibly tall and stiff. A heap of tiny pieces of paper were swept back towards them from under the hedge by the breeze.

'It's amazing the way the wind has changed direction suddenly, isn't it?'

She waited for Albert to echo her thoughts, but there was silence. He sank down into the deckchair and rested his forehead against his hands. Paula thought for one awful moment that he was crying. She put a hand on his shoulder. He lifted up his head and tried to smile.

'It's all right. I suppose I'm making a mountain out of a molehill, but that letter was from my ex-girlfriend.'

'Oh.'

'And it's the last letter I'll ever receive from her.'

Paula's heart thudded. 'Why? Have you broken it off?'

'Yes. I wrote her a proposal last week. It was foolish of me really. I suppose I should have waited until we knew each other a little better, but she turned me down, and it was all in that letter.'

'I am sorry.'

'I suppose I'm sentimental, but I wanted to keep it as a memento.'

'Of course. I think you're being very brave about it.'

'I suppose I've got to face facts.'

'Yes, it's always good to face facts.' Paula smiled at the irony as she heard herself echoing his statement.

'Yes. It is good to face facts, isn't it.'

She began to giggle. This reiteration could go on ad infinitum. She tried to suppress her laughter until tears welled up in her eyes. She rubbed them with her fist.

'I suppose I feel a bit like crying too. You see I was really keen on her.'

He looked at her and Paula suddenly noticed that his eyes were an unusual grey – or perhaps it was their expression which was unusual. They were completely open and candid. His shirt was very white and she realised that she had not met anyone like him for a very long time. She delved into her mind and realised that she had known boys like that back in her childhood, but not since the age of ten. He was curiously uncomplicated.

'I wrote her a book of poems to show her how I felt about her, but I was stupid enough to post the proposal letter before I got round to showing her the poems.'

'Oh, how awful.'

He rummaged in his document case and took out a small book bound in vellum. 'You might like to read some of them.'

She opened the book a third of the way through, apprehensively, forcing herself to keep a straight face, in case it was doggerel. She read the poem slowly and then looked at him in amazement.

'Did you write this?'

'Yes.'

She read the next one.

'Did you really write all these?'

'Yes. Are they any good?'

Paula paused and stared into the grey pupils. She handed him back the book.

'They're very good indeed. What a shame you didn't just...' She paused and sighed.

'I must be off,' he said. 'I've got some telexing to do.'

She stood up with him. The tiny pieces of torn-up paper fluttered around their feet like confetti.

He coughed. 'Look, could you ... I mean ... would you like to come out with me on Saturday?'

Paula gasped and her heart thumped. She liked him so much, but ... She thought very quickly. She weighed

up the pros and cons and could only remember his awful repetitions and Kathy's giggles. She could see Kathy
hunched up in laughter over her desk. *A Cornish pastie...*

She crossed her fingers, all ten of them, behind her
back.

'No, I'm afraid not. I'd like to very much, but I'm
engaged.'

'Oh, I'm very sorry. I didn't realise—'

'It's not really official yet. Actually, it's a secret. Between friends. You won't tell anyone, will you?'

'No.'

'Just between friends.'

He smiled and echoed the words, 'Between friends.'
He stooped slightly and scratched his head. 'Look,
would you like to read the rest of these poems?'

She blinked, and felt a stab of pain in her heart. 'I'd
like to but ... I can't. They're intended for your fiancée
and I feel I'm prying. But do send them to a magazine,
or something.'

He stood up, his tie flapping in the wind. 'That
wouldn't be the same. They're meant to be read by—'

'Good heavens, it's ten to two. I must hurry.'

She ran away from him, zigzagging between the
blocks of coloured glass. A dazzle of pinks and greens.
She ran quickly back to the office, leaping over the
shadows and up the stairs to the room where Kathy was
sitting reading in the sun.

'What are you reading?'

'Keats.' Kathy sprayed her hair with conditioner.
'I'm lost in Keats.'

'Do you like Keats?'

SUSAN NOBLE

'Sometimes I do, sometimes I don't. Most of the time I do. Tell me, did you have any gay repartee with Albert over the hollyhocks?'

Paula hesitated.

'You look very mysterious. Did he propose or something?'

'No,' Paula tried to laugh. She wanted to tell Kathy about the poems and the letter, but she could not take the risk of provoking Kathy's ridicule.

'No, we just looked at the fountains. They've got a special exhibition on. Lots of little mini-fountains, made out of glass in different colours.'

'Sounds hideous.' Kathy flicked over the page of her Keats. 'I must go along tomorrow and see just how ghastly it looks.'

Paula stifled a sigh and laughed heartily.

5   The Change

ANTHONY WALKED along the river-bank until he reached the bench, and stretched himself out full length on his stomach. The planks dug into his vertebrae, but he was too sleepy to care. It was a hot August afternoon. The bees and bluebottles hummed in the long grass by the bank and the slow swish of punts was broken only by shouts from passing undergraduates. It was the last days of term at the end of his first year.

He shut his eyes and felt a deep sense of satisfaction. He has found his feet. Books, tutorials and discussions had dominated his life, and Rosalie – above all, Rosalie. An image formed behind the blackness of his eyelids. A round face with pointed chin, brown eyes and honey-coloured hair. It was an unusual combination and her expression was unusual too, sometimes inquisitive, sometimes wistful, more often than not completely vacant, but within that vacuum, ideas would be formulating.

Anthony was always surprised by the asperity of Rosalie's remarks. It seemed incongruous with her languid eyes and the gentleness of her movements. That morning, for instance, she had told him that he was too complacent.

'I can't be too complacent,' he had said. 'I'm either complacent or I'm not.'

Her lips closed together and her face was totally

blank. 'Everyone is sometimes complacent, but you're complacent all the time.'

'I'm just happy.'

'Good.'

He opened his eyes as an insect brushed against his eyebrows. He flicked it off and then rolled over to see a dead earwig drop on to the grass. He had killed it. Had he thought about it, he would not have done so. He always set himself a high standard of conduct, and was pleased to know that he kept to it as far as possible.

Perhaps this was what she meant by complacency, but surely it was simply self-respect and the natural outcome of his continual attempts to do the right thing. It was as though his willpower were set in the direction of good rather than evil. An image formed in his mind of a television aerial with an angel on one side and devil on the other.

Why was it fashionable to be ashamed of the desire to be good? Was Rosalie turning against him and branding him with the charge of hypocrisy? Other people had done so. He recalled his holiday in Paris the previous summer with Simon, who regarded all women as sexual objects, and who had also scoffed at Anthony.

'You're a bloody Puritan,' he said one day, when they were standing together on a bus. Anthony winced as Simon wolf-whistled – continuously and without discrimination – at every woman sauntering past the bus window. As it reached the Jardins de Luxembourg, three girls in shorts, throwing pebbles into a fountain, screamed with laughter and waved at Simon when he poked his head out of the window.

'Careful, you'll have your head chopped off,' Anthony shouted.

'Bloody Puritan. Sometimes I think you should enter a monastery.'

Anthony had indeed thought about doing just that, but had never done so. Instead he had prayed regularly and focussed his attention on God at all times.

Some grass tickled against his face. He peeped through his fingers at the insects clinging to the grasses and tried to refer the moment to God. His gaze filtered his span of vision to one ant on one blade of grass.

He realised that at this moment he alone of everyone in the world was conscious of this particular ant. He could if he wished kill it, as he had killed the other insect a moment ago. Or he could pluck out the blade of grass and lay it on his knee. Or he could refrain from any action and simply observe.

As he watched, the ant reached the top of the blade of grass and began to descend the other side. The grass was strong and bore the insect's weight casually, only occasionally bending and swaying.

At that moment Anthony felt a sense of peace. He had the gift of faith. If a disaster occurred, his faith would give him courage. There could be a fire in the college hall or a drowning student in the river. He would save the day and walk through the flames or jump into the water. Why should Rosalie mock his faith?

There was a soft rustling of grass. He looked up. It was Rosalie. She smiled. Her head was turned to one side.

'I thought I'd find you here, lazybones. I found this in your pigeonhole.' She handed him a letter. He opened it and read it. His lips drew into a thin line.

'It's from my bank. It's ridiculous. It says I'm overdrawn by fifty pounds. I know I'm not – where's my cheque-book?'

He rummaged in his briefcase for a moment. 'Bother. I've lost it.' He looked at her demandingly. She should be able to help him.

'Perhaps you left it somewhere. Didn't you open it at Mike's the other day, when you were looking for your Kafka? I remember you turned everything out on the sofa.'

Anthony's eyes were squinting with the effort to think. 'I remember! Mike kept playing around with all that stuff and I told him to leave it alone. I thought he put everything back. He's an odd bloke...'

Rosalie raised her left eyebrow.

'There was no-one else in the room at the time.'

Anthony clenched a handful of grass and then kicked out angrily. 'Bloody hell. He's always in debt. He's obviously taken that cheque-book, so what am I supposed to do now?'

'What do you feel you ought to do?' She looked at him quizzically.

'There's no question about it. We'll have to get it back.'

'But he's in debt.'

'I'd like to pay his debts but I can't. I'm sorry, Rosalie, but if he's irresponsible with money, he's got to learn how to manage it. It'll be good for him.'

'Come off it. You know why he's in debt.'

'No.'

'Drugs.'

'Are you sure?'

'Positive. I'm not going to tell you how I know, but I do and I think you ought to forget about the cheque-book. He's up to his neck in debt, and you can always ask your father—'

'You know I can't. It would be against his principles. I'm sorry, but there is a limit.'

'A limit to what?'

Anthony paused as an ant crawled up his arm, and he flicked it off angrily. 'What am I supposed to tell my father?' he said.

'Whatever you like.'

'I'm not going to. I'm going to get the money back from Mike and that's that. I mean, it's impossible.'

Rosalie stood up and pulled him up alongside her.

'Don't try and win me round,' he said. 'The answer is no.'

She stared at him. Her eyes were vacant.

'Well, what sort of explanation can I give my father? I'm not going to tell a lie.'

Her face was completely blank. She stared at something beyond his left shoulder. Her turned round, but there was nothing to see. She opened her bag and wrote out a cheque for £50. She placed it in his hand, as though he were a child, folding his fingers together over the cheque and walked away over to the grass to the path beyond.

Anthony heaved a sigh of relief. In the distance he

could see the swinging of her leather handbag. A trace of her perfume lingered in the air. He realised that the £50 was no loss to her. He would be able to pay her back in his own good time and save Mike's reputation. He was pleased. He wanted to be able to help Mike. The whole affair had turned out for the best.

He lay down on the grass again. His heart was still beating quickly. If only he could relax and regain that tranquillity as before. But as his face brushed against the grass he knew that he was no stronger and no better than anyone else. The image of the college fire and the drowning man arose before his eyes, but this time he could see himself retreating.

Was he a coward? No more than anyone else. He was simply a human being and there were limits. He shut his eyes. Was he cowardly? He did not know. He tried to pray but it was difficult. Shouts and humming broke the silence: there was no peace. Everything was moving and rustling. He tried to make contact with God, amidst his fear and his shock, but he was not sure whether he was really in contact with Him.

He suddenly felt very isolated – but alive.

6   The Turning of the Tables

POLLY AWOKE exhausted on Good Friday bank holiday. Every bone in her body ached. Her eyes were sore, her feet cramped. She shuffled out of bed and turned on the radio full volume, pulling open the curtains. A dazzle of green trees flooded her eyes. She blinked and turned back to the room.

Clothes lay scattered in heaps on armchairs. The dressing table was covered with books and the sideboard was white from the talcum power she had upset the previous morning in her haste to make coffee.

As she walked stiffly around the room she noticed patches of talc all over the place – on the carpet, clinging to a teacloth, even between the pages of her magazines. It was too annoying that Marian had chosen today of all days to visit her for tea, and without even an invitation.

Polly never organised herself properly and this last week had been crammed with activities, each overlapping the next, so she had scarcely had time to fit everything in, let alone clean up the flat.

People often said that twins were telepathic. Perhaps Marian had contrived the visit to gloat at her twin's lack of discipline, for Marian was organised and disciplined to the nth degree.

Polly scooped up her clothes and taking them into the bathroom, dipped them into a bowl of hot, soapy water. It was easy to be organised if one limited oneself, but for Polly there were no limits, no boundaries. She never refused an invitation. She never neglected to read a book through lack of time, nor go to an interesting lecture. Perhaps she was attempting the impossible and the result was chaotic but nevertheless she felt satisfied in a confused sort of way.

It would take at least three hours to clean the flat. She sighed. It was time to call a halt to it all. If the phone rang she would force herself not to answer it. That would be easier than refusing to see somebody or making an excuse.

Just as she had made her decision, the phone began to ring. She ran into the lounge and began to dust and polish and Hoover, still in her dressing-gown. The ringing was persistent. Perhaps it was Dave or Gavin, or even Sheila. But whoever it was, she wasn't going to answer it.

When the ringing finally stopped, she ran back into the bathroom and rinsed out her clothes. It was peaceful, cleaning and washing. The simple functions had restored objects to their former state. In a way it was the essence of living, restoring the ravages of time so that everything reverted to its former state, just as after a night's sleep the body recovers its energy.

She laughed, realising she certainly had not recovered hers. It would take a week of sleep to even begin to recover her normal lively state. But nothing would induce her to reveal her weakness before Marian.

She shrugged. Twins were meant to love each other. In a way they did, but the bond between them used to be torn apart by rivalry until finally it all changed. In the end Marian's slow, steady progression up the ladder of success, her gradual accumulation of qualifications and achievements, had simply exacerbated Polly's contempt for outward success. She had turned to a way of life that was spontaneous, that did not heap success on herself, but forced her to give and share with others.

That was why she never achieved anything. Nothing was ever finished: books and articles were started enthusiastically and then abandoned through lack of time; paintings were begun and never quite completed; her wardrobe was full of cotton dresses and skirts that still needed the final touch.

It was this finishing touch which she always omitted, as though, mesmerised by a new acquisition, she abandoned each previous endeavour. But now, as time passed, and the flat began to look clean and tidy, she felt a peculiar sense of satisfaction. She switched off the radio. It was quiet and all she could hear were the birds singing outside the window.

She looked through the panes. The trees seemed to spread out into an amorphous whole, branch upon branch. There were no limits, no boundaries between them, except for one small elm, delicately shaped and pruned, a perfect specimen.

She walked up to the mirror and gazed at her reflection: streaks of mascara had spread round her eyes. Her lipstick was smudged, so that her mouth looked red and sore and her hair hung in messy curls around her shoulders. She dropped some cleaning lotion on a piece of cotton wool and wiped off the make-up with quick movements.

Her face was white again, not beautiful, not even

pretty, but at least neat and clean. She brushed her hair behind her ears and tied it back with a ribbon – and then blinked: the austere reflection gazing back did not belong to Polly but to Marian. Her heart began to beat faster and she tried to perceive some minute detail that would distinguish her face from Marian's, but it was impossible. The clear white skin and long curve of the cheekbone shone back at her proudly.

She sat down exhausted in an armchair. It was as though Marian had won. Yet she felt a sense of peace. The air was scented from the lavender polish; the carpet was clean. She felt she was part of an orderly plan. She had undertaken one small task – to clean her flat – and had completed it without interruption. She sighed. Perhaps it was time to change her way of living. It did not seem to get her anywhere.

Marian's neat life forced itself upon her vision. She could see Marian and Derek and their two small children, all clean and neatly dressed, with their close circle of friends, and semi-circle of more distant friends and outer circle of acquaintances.

She smiled. Marian would be pleased to see that she had grown out of her adolescent phase at last. It had taken a lot to make Polly think it all out like this. It was merely the aching fatigue from all these late nights that had triggered her resolve, but now she was no longer tired. She felt bright and cheerful.

The doorbell rang. She opened the door and Marian rushed in, followed by her two children. Her hair was dishevelled and hung round her shoulders in a tangle of curls. She was wearing a check smock and jeans and the children were in fancy dress.

Polly gasped. 'Come in,' she said.

The children rushed into the room and started to jump up and down on the chairs.

Marian collapsed onto the carpet by the fire.

'We're exhausted,' she said. 'We've had a hectic day.'

Polly stared open-mouthed.

'We've all taken up painting recently. A friend of Derek's got us interested in it and we discovered that we've all got quite a flair, particularly Jenny.'

The little girl rubbed her fist against a green streak of paint on her cheek.

'It's great fun,' said Marian, 'but terribly time-consuming. God, I'm exhausted.' She shut her eyes and began to dose.

Polly looked at her. She had patches of mascara beneath her eyes and her lipstick was so smudged it made her mouth look sore. Her hair was messy and as her head nodded she had a perplexed expression as though there were something she was trying to recall or to complete; then, as if realising it was impossible, she fell asleep.

7   The Wedding Dress

ANNAH PAUSED in front of an antique bookstall and pushed her hair behind her ears. It hung over her long pink coat like the branches of a willow tree.

Pauline sighed. Why did Hannah always wear such trailing coats? This one had a crooked hem and a large safety pin was gleaming through the fold on the left.

Her criticism of Hannah extended only to her clothes, however. She looked up at Hannah's beaming face.

'Books,' she squealed. 'Masses and masses of books. Look, Annie. This looks like your cup of tea.'

She handed Annie a brown tooled volume of nineteenth-century poetry. Annie began to flick through it, thumbing each page wetly and grinning hugely.

Pauline sighed again. She did not usually take a strong dislike to people, but for some reason Annie irritated her. She tried to decide whether it was the continual smile she disliked or her slow, non-stop conversations. She felt ashamed. Annie was in her mid-forties and was what most people would term 'a good-hearted soul'.

At that moment Annie grinned at her. 'I like this one,' she said and began to recite Wordsworth slowly.

'What's the matter? Have you got a headache?' she asked as Pauline put her hand to her head.

'I think I'll walk back towards the street a bit to get

some air,' said Pauline. 'I feel a bit faint.'

She hated herself for the lie. It was not faintness but irritability.

She walked slowly past the rows of stalls in the antique market. On one stall, among the gold brushes and combs and tiny pocket mirrors with lacy gold edges, studded with beads, a porcelain chess-set attracted her attention.

She fingered the pawns and realised, as she moved the piece on the far left forward, what the reason was for her irritability. Something had zigzagged across her view of life that evening.

Her unified concept of the universe, of God, of the rightness of things, had been dislodged by her dislike of people. The hatred and criticism which she felt for so many people loomed in her head like a large muddy pool and she felt that she was sinking beneath the mud.

Why this contempt, this bitterness? No-one would suspect that beneath her cool expression she had caught a glimpse of herself in a gold-framed oval mirror that hung from silver chains. A pale girl in a green shirt-waister with long, pale, ginger hair. Her skin was white and her eyebrows were nonexistent. She looked almost like an albino in the shadows.

As she moved she caught a flash of her real self behind the paleness. Her eyes were tiny and grey, and the pupil glinted slightly. She stared for a long time at the pinpoints in them, trying to reason with her reflection, but the coloured shape in the glass stared back coldly, with hatred.

Pauline walked on until she reached a dress stall,

and noticed in the middle a white lace dress with long sleeves and a gold belt. Perhaps it was an old wedding-dress and she suddenly conceived the idea of buying it and wearing it that evening. As she handed over a small wad of notes she wondered whether she could sponge out the blackness inside her by wearing the dress for a couple of hours. She slipped it over her head on top of her skirt and blouse.

'You're not going to wear that now?' asked the girl behind the stall. 'It'll get really dirty – these pavements are filthy.'

'I don't mind,' said Pauline. 'I've always been eccentric.'

'Eccentric! You're telling me,' said the girl and nudged in the ribs the man at the next stall. 'Did you hear that, Jim? The young lady's going to walk round the market in her wedding dress.'

Pauline adjusted the belt so that the end of the gold chain hung down to the left of the dress.

'It fits you like a glove.'

'Very fashionable madam,' said Jim.

Pauline giggled and walked along the road a little further. By this time she had reached the edge of the market and could feel the fresh air from the park opposite. She turned right into a row of large white mansion houses and hotels. In the distance she could see a crowd of people in long dresses and hats, throwing confetti. She giggled to herself at the thought of peeping on a wedding crowd in her wedding dress.

She tiptoed towards the edge of the crowd and nearly tripped over an elderly man with a white stick.

'Can I help you across the road?' she said automatically.

He laughed – a feeble, coughing sound. 'Helping old Uncle George as usual, even on your wedding day. Yes, you may help me across, my dear.' He shuffled over the road with tiny steps.

'But I'll tell you this and you'll regret not taking me advice. He's a layabout. Does nothing but write really and play his banjo, or whatever you care to call it, and in six months' time you'll be sick of the sight of him. I know his sort. He nearly knocked me over while I was walking down the high street last Wednesday. Lazy good-for-nothing, he is.'

'Yes, Uncle George,' said Pauline.

A woman in a large pink hat rushed up to him.

'Come along, George. You want to say goodbye to Alison, before she goes off.'

'I've just been talking to her.'

'Don't talk rubbish. She's over by the best man.'

'I've just been giving her my opinion about—'

'George, you've had too much to drink.'

Pauline slipped away, feeling ashamed. Tricking a blind man. It was cruel. He must have had just enough sight to glimpse the white dress. She made her way back towards the market in time to see Hannah and Annie walking away from the last stalls, their bags full of books and other purchases. When Hannah spotted Pauline, she shrieked with laughter.

'My God, you look hilarious!' She nudged Annie, who turned around, mouth open in amused astonishment.

'Pauline, you're a scream!'

They both began humming Mendelssohn's wedding march as the wind began to blow her dress around her legs.

'More like the ice maiden than love's young dream,' Hannah giggled a little cruelly.

'I wish I could know, I wish I could know,' Pauline muttered to herself, but this just made Hannah and Annie laugh even more hysterically.

'Goodness, you really are cold,' Hannah said as she felt Pauline's hands.

'Don't look so worried,' said Annie. 'Whatever it is, it's not worth worrying about.'

Pauline sighed and let go her hold of the problem. The wedge of hatred would have to stay within her for the time being.

'Must powder my nose,' said Annie. 'I've been laughing so much I've taken all the powder off. Can you lend me a mirror somebody?'

Pauline lifted a square pocket mirror out of her handbag and looked in it quickly before handing it to Annie.

'All is vanity,' said Hannah.

Pauline giggled.

'Vanity? I'm a ginger albino!'

'You're still vain with it. Look at your face,' Hannah replied.

Pauline laughed again. What she had seen pleased her. The pinpoints in the pupils had vanished and the eyes were a clear, transparent grey.

8   The Return

KARL WAS apprehensive about revisiting his birthplace, a district that had been ravaged by war and now in the process of reconstruction. It seemed sentimental and yet necessary, as though completing a circle of gold rings, one of which has been broken by the force of circumstance.

He had left the town, a hundred kilometres from Warsaw, several years before the war at the age of eight, and since then had rarely visualised it in his mind – a defence mechanism to block out the painful reminder of his family, who had all perished during the war, all in different ways.

Only occasionally did he for an instant cast his mind back upon the region with its dull houses and narrow streets. The predominant memory was of a grey ugliness, and it had only been a chance business trip to Warsaw that had prompted this return visit. He now worked for a button firm in London and had been sent to an international trade conference, which had ended the previous day.

As he walked down the empty street, surrounded on one side by buildings still in the process of reconstruction and on the other by a series of large half-completed office blocks, he was surprised to feel no pang of nostalgia, no painful recollections, nor was he conscious of the numbness that comes with an experience that one does not wish to face. Instead he only felt calm indifference as he walked briskly down the grey pavements, the sound of his footsteps ringing out with harsh clarity in the cold February mid-morning.

He was surprised that he did not meet a single person. Even the office blocks seemed devoid of construction workers. He felt oddly vacant and began to wonder whether the visit had been conceived in a moment of sentimentality, and as he emerged at the other end of the street, he was feeling a flat sense of anti-climax.

As he crossed the road he noticed the carcase of a bird, mangled by a passing car, lying by the kerbside. As he looked at it he did not feel the usual sense of revulsion. The dead bird somehow represented everything about his early childhood in Poland that he had been trying unsuccessfully to recall, and which now overwhelmed him.

Tears gushed down his cheeks and dripped onto his raincoat as he stood, slightly stooped and with head bowed, staring at the bloodstained remnants of flesh. He was unable to straighten himself or even crouch down by the bird, but remained bowed in a question-mark stance over the spot, as if paralysed.

After several minutes he slowly straightened himself up and made his way to the railway station. As he reached the station entrance the sun began to shine so that, despite the cold, the whole scene took on a spring-like appearance.

He peeped into the dingy interior of the station and, changing his mind, turned left and made his way down a long narrow lane to visit the farm, which he recalled from his youth. During the twenty-minute walk the sun seemed to shine brighter and brighter, so that his grief was obliterated by the overwhelming light of the sun.

He entered a cornfield to the right of the farm and walked unsteadily through the middle of it. The sheaves of corn stood up bright yellow in the sunlight, leaning at an angle of forty-five degrees, so that gazing at it, he had an odd sensation of dizziness. The sweep of the corn caught him up in a circle of movements so that, suddenly invigorated, he ran headlong through the corn, until he tripped over a long stump, jutting out at an angle, so that he lay huddled in the corn. Grief mingled with joy overcame him and unable to express the tension, he stood up and ran back out of the field.

Just as he reached the exit, two butterflies appeared a few inches away from his nose. They clapped their wings together in feeble combat and eventually fluttered away over his head and into the distance. For no apparent reason this made him feel completely calm and serene, as though the contest of the butterflies had purged the tension within him between grief and joy, and the forces of life had for some invisible reason been cancelled.

He returned to the station, walking with slow, regular steps and tranquil features as he caught the train back to Warsaw.

9   Shadow Dance

LUCY SAT nibbling crisps, abstracted. She picked at each crisp with rhythmic regularity, her face expressing neither happiness nor sadness as she ate, her left elbow resting casually on two pieces of screwed-up sugar paper. Her gaze remained fixed as Gerald sat down to her right, noisily removed the dirty pile of crockery from his table and placed his bag clumsily on a nearby chair.

'I've seen you before, haven't I?' he said eagerly, as if ignoring her obviously cocooned indifference.

'Probably,' she replied. 'I've been attending classes here for some time.'

'Oh, which ones do you go to?' he asked enthusiastically.

She stifled a sigh and peeled the top of a yoghurt carton, 'Three – art history, creative writing and playing the piano.'

'That's a lot,' he said as though an intelligent remark had elicited a friendly response.

'You think so?' She dipped her spoon into her yoghurt.

For several minutes she continued to eat nonchalantly in silence, while Gerald gulped down his food and scratched his head, desperately trying to prolong the conversation.

'Are you married?' he asked casually.

She turned away, annoyed. 'Why do you keep asking

me questions?'

He flinched, suddenly aware of the hostility he had been trying not to recognise; at the same time she turned and looked at him closely and frankly.

'No ... I mean yes, I was, but I'm not now.'

He sighed, relieved that the barrier between them had apparently disappeared. 'I thought you were – I mean, I thought you had been.'

She immediately stiffened. 'So what's that supposed to mean? Do I look married or something?'

'Yes, in a way. You've got a married look.'

She laughed, amused at his naïveté. 'I suppose I do look married. And you – are you married?'

'No.'

She moved her chair towards him a little, gazed at him with curiosity and asked, 'And what do you do?'

It was Gerald's turn to be irritated by the question, but he concealed it. 'I live.'

She laughed. 'And what's that supposed to mean?'

'Anything you like.'

'But what do you do all day?' she persisted inquisitively.

'I read, I paint. I write. I eat. I sleep. Nothing much.'

'It sounds like a lot of hard work.'

He detected a note of surprise, even sympathy in her voice.

Lucy, suddenly aware that she was revealing some warmth, immediately grew cold again and looked at her watch.

'My class begins soon,' she said, and moved away from the table.

10   Indifference

MY REGRET is that I did not join my father, when he ventured out alone. He was a botanist and used to visit distant country spots as part of his work routine. At the time I never realised that he craved for the company of his family.

Sometimes his nearest neighbour would be sixteen miles away and my father would spend several days and nights at a time camping in lonely spots, identifying and classifying unusual species of plants. I only realised in later years, from reading his diary and worknotes, that his solitude was not desirable to him, but merely endured.

In rejecting his occasional suggestions that I should join him on these trips, I was performing a calculated act of coldness. My mother had died in my infancy and my two brothers were considerably older than myself. Both were involved in professional activities at the time when my father's fieldwork was at its peak.

My indifference to him was not the result of obstinacy or contrariness in myself, provoked by positive seeking for affection. Nor was it fostered by any overt or latent incestuous desire on either side. For he was a quiet, moderate man, self-contained and above all things reasonable.

It was his very reasonableness that made my indifference to him so critical for me, since I knew that my actions would be analysed and that the only conclusion that could be reached from him was that I simply did not love him. Nor was my indifference the result of any violent love or hatred for him. It was rather a direct act of will, a conscious choosing of the evil path, the decision to take on the reins of hatred.

Yet this appeared to be contrary to my whole approach to life, which was that actions and achievements could only be attained by the power of love. In my continual advocacy of love as a dynamic electricity I was in fact acting against my own nature, for my temperament seems to be inherently cold and unresponsive.

People are often deceived because the experiences of my life and the contact which I have gained with certain dynamic personalities has resulted in my having a tremendous superficial warmth and vitality.

On looking back at my attitude to my father I perceive that I wanted the one person whose love for me made him vulnerable to my indifference. All the same, this fact is a clear indication to me that the good opinion that people hold concerning my attitude and character is meaningless, for I alone know the contortions which I have performed in order to discover who I am and to become myself.

It was only the fact that after my father died I had a sustained relationship with someone who was inherently good, that I managed to attain contact with the good forces of life, and through this agency my wheels have now swivelled into the right gear.

11   Cousins

L EAVES RUSTLED against the ground and swirled against Sally's shoes as she walked briskly down St Giles on an autumn afternoon. She surveyed the wide road ahead of her. It was practically deserted except for two dons who stood chatting inside the porter's lodge of a small nearby college.

On Sunday afternoons the back streets always seemed cold and empty, yet this emptiness had a protective quality. It was a relief to Sally, who hated crowds and noise, to be able to walk and walk as far as she liked, in the cold silence.

A gust of air behind her left ear made her shiver; she pulled her gown tighter round her like a cocoon. She looked slightly comical, bundled up in the black cotton folds, her long legs pink because of the damp gust of wind and her long hair blowing back behind her neck as she strode breathlessly down the road.

School was behind her; in front of her was the prospect of two and a half years of university. The freedom of it all was overwhelming. Sally began to run as she turned over the idea in her mind. So much had happened in the past three months since her nineteenth birthday.

She ran faster and faster. A stream of yellow sunlight turned the brown leaves to copper and red. Hedges glowed and college quadrangles flashed by, emerald green with pools of light flickering over them.

People began to pass, in groups, in pairs, or on their own. Snatches of conversation flew past her. She took in deep gulps of air: she felt purged and purified as she ran along the streets.

Emptiness and solitude, the opportunity to expand and develop her ideas in the autumn silence. Her imagination began to contort and swell like a snake casting off its old skin. It seemed that every colour and every sensation was intensified. She had trodden on a heap of desiccated leaves that crunched into dust like gigantic cornflakes.

As she approached Geraldine's college the light grew more and more gingery so that the people emerging from the college gate seemed to have coppery hair.

She slowed her steps as she entered the quadrangle and tried to collect her thoughts. Geraldine was her second cousin and between them there existed a mixture of affection and rivalry. Within the family the rivalry was dominant, but outside it the link of blood ties would assert itself.

Sally envied Geraldine her academic success; she admired her political convictions and her enormous energy. Yet simultaneously she despised what she saw as her phoneyness, her posing. Geraldine, sensing this, would greet her warmly with a carefully measured condescension. But Sally ignored this barrier between them, and on Sunday afternoons she would be eager to join her tea parties and, sitting on a cushion by the fire, would listen with interest to the heated weekly discussions.

Sally knocked on the door with a sense of expectancy,

a conviction that she was about to be agreeably entertained. Her two knocks echoed in the passageway and she was so preoccupied with listening to the echoes that it took her several moments to realise that there was no reply.

She knocked again and said, 'Hello? Can I come in?'

There was still no reply. She pushed open the door and blinked as she entered the darkened room. The curtains were still drawn and a heavy odour of burnt-out joss sticks lingered in the air.

The room was full of people but there was no sound. They were simply sitting there, with heads lolling slightly from the warmth of the gas fire. Sally's fingers began to tingle as she sat down in the corner. After a moment or two, she realised they were not, in fact, sitting in silence, but listening to a record and she managed to perceive the sound of a harp.

As she listened she surveyed the group. Familiar faces and familiar clothes. In front of her sat Tam, wearing an Arran sweater. Somehow it seemed appropriately matched to the lilting sound of the harp. She scrutinised its ribbed patterns of thick beige wool. Tam scratched his head and tufts of curly hair sprang back as he did so. The hair was the colour of sand and each hair on his head seemed to vibrate slightly in response to the music.

Geraldine turned up the volume of the record player. Her long, gawky figure looked slightly out of place in the neatly arranged room. She kicked a cushion out of the way with her right leg and somehow managed to fold the left leg under her right knee. Geraldine was always contorting herself into strange shapes.

Sally felt almost invisible as she sat in the corner surveying the scene as her cold fingers were thawing in the overheated room and she felt almost as though she had no substance. People shifted to and fro but nobody spoke or communicated.

It seemed to Sally that there was no past, no future: just this moment of being.

These Sunday afternoons continued in a desultory fashion during Sally's last year. Sometimes there would be long discussions and arguments, and Sally would sit back and scrutinise them all without participating.

'Haven't you any opinions, Sally?' Geraldine would ask in exasperation.

'No, I have no opinions,' Sally would reply.

Geraldine would shrug her shoulders and launch into a political harangue.

Sally prided herself on the fact that she was intuitive and she would try to glean moments of insight when she met people.

One day, when they met in the corridor of their college, Geraldine asked her why she was so aloof. 'You'll regret it later,' she added.

'I don't know,' Sally replied. 'I suppose I'm trying to find something.'

They walked slowly down the corridor, swerving to

avoid the porters carrying trunks that had belatedly arrived for the overseas students.

Geraldine laughed. 'That's terribly original. I must remember that.'

Sally had begun to distrust Geraldine and eventually ceased her Sunday afternoon visits. As the terms passed, she became increasingly involved with her own affairs, dividing her time equally between her studies, social engagements and friends, and the freedom and exhilaration she had felt in her first few months at college had long worn off.

One day in her third year, as she was sitting in her room writing an essay by the window, she saw Geraldine running through the quadrangle. By now Sally was considerably more placid than she had been in her first term, but as she looked down at the tall, slim figure leaping down the path, for a moment she felt a stab of nostalgia.

But then she took in Geraldine's blue jeans, the red sweater and untidy black hair and realised that she now represented disorder and lack of discipline for her. She promptly forgot all about Geraldine and returned to her studies with renewed complacency.

She had a large desk diary and an elaborate filing system and her revision plans were carefully organised. She had grown more confident and talkative, while maintaining her need for orderliness. Her conversation was never stimulating, rarely original and was completely lacking in spontaneity, but she became accepted by a small group of like-minded students.

Geraldine, meanwhile, had become involved in student

protest; she had joined a Marxist group and was writing for an underground newspaper.

One Sunday afternoon in the January of her final year, Sally bumped into Geraldine at the porter's lodge. She was surrounded by suitcases and packages and had just booked a taxi.

'Where are you going at this time of the year?' Sally asked.

'I've been sent down,' said Geraldine.

Sally stared at her.

'Actually, I'm rather glad. I'm not in the mood for doing any exams this year.'

Sally detected behind her bravado a look of anxiety.

'I must go,' Geraldine said as the taxi was just arriving.

'I'll give you a hand,' said Sally, lifting up the cases and giving them to the taxi driver. She felt a strange emptiness, sending that a section of her life had just ended.

Geraldine put the final bag into the back of the taxi and climbed in. As she sat back on the seat, she opened the window and tried to smile out at Sally. Her face was very pale and the heavy mascara and lipstick, applied too hastily, gave her grinning face the appearance of a grotesque clown. Sally wondered why her hair was wet.

'Goodbye,' said Geraldine.

Sally continued speculating on the cause of the wet hair for no particular reason and it was only when the taxi had disappeared round the corner that she began to feel frightened, but she could not explain to herself what was behind this fear.

Exams came and passed and Sally emerged with adequate success to effusive approbation from her family. Geraldine meanwhile had taken a teaching post in Spain and only returned to England for brief visits.

A year after Sally came down from Oxford she got married and a few months later took a job teaching in a girls' grammar school in Reading. She had applied for the post because its routine and orderly nature seemed perfectly suited to her temperament.

One Sunday afternoon in autumn when her husband was away on a business trip, she was walking through a small churchyard near the school. It was a cold day and the grass was still damp with traces of rain from the evening before.

A man was sitting on a bench in the graveyard. He began to cough and continued to do so for several minutes. Despite her normal aloofness, Sally walked across the graveyard and offered him a cherry-flavoured drop. He laughed and between fits of coughing fastidiously inserted it between his teeth. He breathed for a moment or two and the coughing ceased.

Sally smiled. She tried to recall something but could not remember what it was. She screwed up her face in her efforts to recall it. He looked at her and mimicking her, scratched his head with a perplexed expression on his face.

'What have you forgotten?' he said.

Sally looked at his curly hair and Arran sweater and laughed, clapping her hands with relief.

'It's all right – I've remembered it now. It's not the perfect weather for sitting in graveyards,' she added.

'Then why don't you go indoors?' he asked.

'Because I like the wind.'

'Poetic but unpractical,' he replied.

Sally sighed. She surveyed him with her usual scrutiny. He was in his mid-forties and had a small grey pointed beard. He could have been the father of one of her pupils. It was only the Arran sweater and curly hair that had reminded her of Tam and of the past; otherwise he was neat, respectable and civilised.

She handed him the packet of cough pastilles. 'Do have these,' she said. 'I don't need them.'

'You don't need them?'

'No, I never get coughs, actually.'

'Then why do you keep them in your bag?'

'Just to be on the safe side.'

He laughed and a little while later Sally walked out of the graveyard.

Back home Sally was feeling restless and decided to go to London. She wanted to mix with crowds of people and noise. The silence and tranquillity was oppressing her. She took the train to Paddington and then the underground to Leicester Square. As she stepped off the train, she bumped into a man and woman talking and laughing. Sally, automatically embarrassed by their lack of restraint, moved away slightly. A hand tapped her on the shoulder. She flinched, and looking up politely, saw that it was Geraldine.

'Good heavens,' said Sally. 'I didn't recognise you.'

Geraldine looked much older, and broader, and was arm in arm with a tall Japanese man, who looked slightly younger than her. Sally laughed at the incongruity of the pair, and Geraldine, immediately perceiving the cause of her amusement, laughed back.

And as Sally stared at the untidy, weather-beaten appearance of her cousin, she felt as though a tremendous burden had been lifted from her. It seemed to her at that instant that Geraldine had lived for the moment and had failed, and that she herself had lived for the future, and had also failed, but surrounded as they were by crowds of people milling around them in noisy groups, she was conscious only of their vitality and enthusiasm. Colours emerged and fragmented beneath the station lights and Sally's attention was riveted by the brass buttons on the jacket of the Japanese man.

As the roar of the trains drowned her thoughts and there seemed to be only movement and pushing, shoving and jostling, Sally realised that for years she had been seeking quietness and solitude, and wondered whether chaos and noise were not perhaps the natural state of affairs.

Geraldine smiled at her but in her smile there was no fear. Only amusement and curiosity. Sally tried to assume an expression that would answer this curiosity, but she had no reply to Geraldine's unspoken question. She did not know what she was or what she was looking for, and so shelving the question, Sally simply scrutinised the scene, with all its noise and colour, and shrugging her shoulders, smiled back.

12   The Painting

JILL KNOCKED on the door of the flat. It was opened by a tall girl with a towel round her head.

'I've come about the room to let.'

'Oh yes,' replied the girl vaguely. 'Do come in. My name's Harriet Gunnersmith.'

She beckoned Jill through the hall and Jill tried to stifle a giggle. The flat was so cluttered: two bicycles were lodged in the hall corridor and piles of books and sheet music littered the carpet.

Harriet sat down at the kitchen table and pulled up a chair for Jill.

'The room is very small and poky. I'm only charging two pounds a week for it.'

'That's all right. I don't need much space.'

'It's got mice too, I'm afraid.'

Jill laughed. 'You'd make a very bad businesswoman.'

'I'm just being honest. And I think I ought to warn you that it might be haunted. That's why my last tenant moved out.'

'The flat belongs to you, I take it?'

'Yes. It was left to me by my great aunt.' She pointed to a painting on the wall of the kitchen. The face was small and pale with curly black hair and insignificant features.

'She looks like you,' said Jane, staring at the painting. The mouth was strange: it seemed to move slightly in the light, like the *Mona Lisa*.

'It's a self-portrait,' said Harriet. 'She was a painter, you see.' She stood up. 'You can move in whenever you like.'

'I'll do it at the weekend, if that's OK. I think I'd better be going though, as I've got an appointment.'

'Here's the key.'

Harriet smiled and as she continued to dry her hair, Jill again noticed the resemblance between her new landlady and the picture on the wall: it was something to do with the flickering mouth.

'You won't be seeing much of me,' said Harriet. 'I'm out most of the time at evening classes.'

When Jill moved into the flat at the weekend she found that, despite all Harriet's warnings, the room was far from unpleasant. It was long and narrow, but quite spacious, and she could find no traces of mice – or ghosts.

She rarely saw Harriet. They would occasionally meet at the breakfast table. One morning Harriet was buttering toast when she looked up at Jill and said, 'You're a contented person.'

'How do you know?'

'I'm intuitive about people. Actually, you'll be surprised to hear this, but I'm psychic. I inherited it from my great aunt. My right ear goes red whenever somebody is talking about me.'

Jane giggled and inwardly labelled Harriet an eccentric.

One morning Harriet tapped her on the shoulder as she was leaving for work.

'Don't be too upset if something happens today, will you?'

Jill looked puzzled and then smiled. 'No.' She hurried off to work and cheerfully told her fellow secretaries what Harriet had said.

'Well, we'll all be on guard for a tragedy of some sort.'

The day passed uneventfully. One of Jill's letters was returned to her by the supervisor because of a misspelling.

'Perhaps that's your disaster of the day,' joked Ros.

'Perhaps.'

Jill was always upset by her mistakes. To console herself she went to the cinema with a friend in the evening and returned to the flat at midnight. The two bicycles were parked in the hall corridor as usual. She went into the kitchen and switched on the light.

Sitting at the table was a man, slumped forward, with a knife in his back.

She looked up at the picture. It looked at her. The mouth slowly smiled three times.

13   The Discovery

ANDREA STOOD apprehensively outside the front-door of the house in Notting Hill Gate. This was the first time she had been to an encounter group. As she peered through the large bay window to her left, half hidden by overgrown weeds, her anxiety was tempered by scepticism. What or whom was she supposed to be encountering and why should it matter?

The door was ajar. She pushed it gently and then walked through the open door to the left of the entrance hall into the front room. A group of around twelve men and women between the ages of twenty and thirty were sitting bare-footed around the room on cushions.

'Hello, you must be Andrea,' said a tall man, dressed entirely in black, fingering his black beard as he spoke. 'Come and sit on a cushion. You can leave your coat and shoes in the corner.'

Andrea obeyed and sat between a Chinese man and an Indian woman.

'I'm Tim,' continued the man with the beard.

'Why do you feel it is necessary to keep telling everyone your name?' said a thin woman in the corner. 'You think you're so bloody important, Tim.'

'I'm not important, Jenny. I'm simply an individual like each one of you and we all have names, so I believe we should use them.'

'Oh, go to hell,' said Jenny.

'Come and sit in the middle of the circle, Jenny.'

She crawled into the middle with her cushion and sat on it cross-legged like a Buddha.

'What are you thinking at this moment, Jenny? What's your attitude to this newcomer?'

'No attitude, I just think, hell it's another bloody person I've got to be polite to.'

'Are you feeling angry, Jenny?'

'No, Tim, I'm just sick of your playing God with all of us.'

Andrea stared at the two of them, hurling insults at each other and began to giggle.

'And I wish she'd stop laughing at me,' Jenny shouted, throwing a cushion at Andrea. It landed by her feet and Andrea felt an uncontrollable urge to laugh. She stared at Tim's solemn black eyes, and heaved convulsively.

'Why are you laughing, Diane?'

'This is so funny.'

'What's funny? I don't think you're feeling anything at the moment. You're just observing us all.'

'I'm observing you all and I feel I'm participating at the same time and the incongruity of it all makes me laugh.'

'Do you really find it funny, Andrea? Do you feel anything at all? What do you feel?'

'Amused.'

'All right, laugh away. Laugh as much as you like.'

Diane tried to laugh but as soon as Tim had said that, her laughter drained away.

'Come on, laugh. Enjoy yourself.'

'I can't. It's not funny.'

He stared at her and plucked a hair from his beard. 'I think you laugh to escape from reality, so that you don't need to feel anything. What are you feeling now?'

'I'm feeling hostile to Jenny and I don't think I trust you.'

'Why not, Andrea?'

'Because you can't just make value judgments about people when you don't even know them.'

'Perhaps it's easier to judge people when you don't know them.'

Andrea thought about this for a few moments and nodded slowly. Her smile faded completely and she knew that he was right.

Half an hour later Andrea was staring at a spot on the ceiling. The cushion was digging into her back. Her body was curved over it on the floor, like a snake writhing around a trapped frog. She breathed deeper and deeper until loud groans were emitted from her chest uncontrollably.

'Stay with the breathing,' said Tim, walking around the bodies that lay strewn all over the carpet of the large bare room.

'Breathe deeper and deeper, until you feel you have reached something and then stay with it.'

Andrea began to go hot and cold. Sweat dripped down her face and she felt giddy. Blood was whizzing round her head, thumping in her ears. Little gold spots began to prick up in front of her eyes. They danced around the electric light bulb on the ceiling.

Flashes and humming, groaning and breathing. Hot and cold. She felt a wave of fatigue. It slapped her in the face, as though a door had been banged against her at her approach. Just to sink into nothingness. To fall, down, down, deep down, where there were no more problems.

'While you're looking at a point on the ceiling, I want you to ask yourself the question, "What do I want out of life?" Just think it over.'

Hot and cold sweat continued to drip down her face. The answer was so priggish: she wanted to be good.

The man next to her sat up and doubled over, beating his head against the carpet.

Everyone looked up. 'Forget about Barry. Just stay with what you are involved in at the moment,' said Tim.

Andrea curled up in a foetal position, buried her head in the cushion and shut her eyes. Black velvet in front of her eyelids. Complete peace. A moment of serenity. It was so obvious that she wanted to laugh. She had been asked a question and she had found the answer straight away.

In the corner, a girl started screaming. 'I hate you, I hate hate you! I hate you! Leave me alone! I hate you! I can't see you! Never visit me again! Go away from me!'

Her head sank deeper and deeper into the cushion. She was bathed in perspiration. It was like coming out of a sauna. It wrinkled down her body like salt water.

A hand prodded her on the shoulder. She looked up and saw Tim's face. She shut her eyes. She did not like his posturing smile. She opened them again and looked straight up into the huge black eyes and enormous black head. He looked remote and benevolent, like an uncle from her childhood.

'Wake up. I want to do something with the group.' He stood up. 'Get into a circle again.'

Slowly the contorted limbs and screams began to subside into normality. Everyone sat on their cushions in a circle.

Tim sat in the corner and looked slowly around the room. Andrea felt angry: she felt she was being manipulated and that, just as Jenny had said, Tim was playing God.

The girl who had been screaming 'I hate you' began to giggle, as Andrea herself had done earlier.

'Maureen, why are you laughing?'

'This is ridiculous. The whole set-up.'

'In what way is it ridiculous?'

'It's not real. It's not a real thing at all. We're all just playing around.'

'Were you being honest when you shouted "I hate you"?'

'I don't know.'

'Come and sit in the middle of the circle, Maureen.'

She got up reluctantly and sat down with crossed legs. She was short and plump with broad shoulders and long, red hair. Her features were large and vacant.

'Barry, climb on Maureen's back.'

Barry got up sheepishly and half sat on top of Maureen.

'Jonathan, climb on Barry's back,' said Tim. 'Now Anne, climb on Jonathan's back.'

Andrea looked up, intrigued. Maureen was bent double. Her face was white.

'Stay with it a minute. Look at yourself, Maureen. This is what you do to yourself all the time. You give in to people. You let them use you. That's why you hate them and that's why you don't really know how you feel.'

She remained motionless.

'So how do you feel now, Maureen? Do you still hate men?'

'I don't know.'

Andrea slipped out of the room, into the next-door annexe. She felt that Tim was phoney. Something in his voice was not quite right. It was not the role of the group that was false. It was his manipulation of it.

She put on her coat and looked around the room for her bag. Then she realised that somebody had broken the window and glass shards littered the floor as she walked round. Black night flooded in through the broken window. She shivered and leaving the centre, ran down the road,

Twenty minutes later she was back in her bedsitter. She switched on the three lamps and the electric fire and sat down on the rug to think.

Tim would be annoyed that she had left. She looked at her watch. It was a quarter to twelve. The group would probably have finished by now, Yet she didn't want to sleep. Her fatigue had departed and in its place she was feeling curious.

Something was puzzling her: it was to do with the broken window. She had looked at the cotton-wool blackness outside and shivered. Why? Because it seemed as though there was nothing left in the world, as though once people had been categorised and psychoanalysed, the rest was all fantasy, and the black sky had mocked her naïve optimism. She felt as though everyone was playing a sophisticated game at living and she alone was unaware of the rules.

Tim has scoffed at Maureen's inclination to give herself to other people. But to come out on top, to manage others. What did it all mean? She shut her eyes and tried to retrieve the black velvet. Slowly, as the warmth of the fire muzzled her forehead, she began to thaw out, to think in slow patterns. There were people who succeeded and there were idealists and some people were fortunate enough to combine the two.

She reached out a hand and switched on the radio. It was one of Bach's Brandenberg concertos – she recognised it was something her Uncle Paul used to play on the violin when she was young.

It was odd: that was the second time she had thought about Uncle Paul that night. She recalled Tim's face with its look of benevolence. The eyes were almost hypnotic and yet they were not familiar. They were penetrating but aloof. It was a curious combination.

There was a knock at the door. She shuddered violently with shock: it was five to twelve. Perhaps it was the landlady with a complaint. She stood up unsteadily and opened the door. It was Tim.

'Can I come in?'

'Yes.'

He sat down on a chair and yawned. 'I'm sorry to disturb you so late, but I thought you'd still be up.'

She sat down on the rug again and stared at him blankly.

'Why did you walk out of the group tonight?'

'I agreed with Maureen. It wasn't real. You're using people.'

He stared at her. It was a look of deep condescension.

'There's something that you're hiding, Andrea. What are you hiding?'

She stood up. 'I don't feel like any more of all this jargon.'

He flushed angrily. 'To hell with your bloody-mindedness. You're afraid of something. What is it? What is the thing in your whole life that frightened you the most?'

She yawned and stared at the fire. The bars were orange, long orange rods like elongated red lollies, except that they would freeze you to numbness with fire.

'Think very hard. In your whole life, what was the most deeply frightening experience?'

She rubbed her eyes. 'I can't bear amateur psychoanalysis. It's nauseating. What's the point of looking into people's minds? You're just creating things that aren't there.'

'It's you who create them, Andrea.'

'And I do wish you wouldn't keep calling me Andrea every other word. It's so creepy.'

He stroked her hair and she retreated from his touch.

'I hate you.'

'I think you're very frightened. Tell me the most frightening moment in your life.'

She sighed, realising that there was no point in trying to resist the question. She thought for a long time.

'One Christmas, when I was sixteen, we were all in the dining-room at home, having Christmas dinner. There was my close family and Uncle Paul and Aunt Brenda.'

Tim listened.

'I think Uncle Paul had drunk a bit too much. It was so stupid: he started to quarrel with my brother. It was all to do with modern art. We all sat there in silence and then Uncle Paul threw his dinner plate on the floor. It broke into three pieces and all the turkey and sprouts slithered over the carpet.

'My mother started to cry and the rest of us just sat there in silence. I was very frightened … And you look a little like Uncle Paul.'

He nodded – was it a nod of comprehension or was he just putting on what he thought was the correct expression?

'I see. You expect families to be happy and cosy. You expect life to be happy and cosy. You were lying on the floor quite contentedly tonight, thinking how pleasant everything was and then you realised that life is very complicated.

'Now I want you to pretend that I'm your Uncle Paul. Do something to me. Do anything you like. Hit me. Throw a book at me.'

She stared at him open-mouthed. 'I can't.'

'Let yourself.'

'I really can't.'

'Do something!' he shouted.

There was a banging on the ceiling from the flat above.

'Shhh! You'll wake up all the neighbours.'

She picked up a book and tapped it gently on his head.

'The trouble is, I've just realised that you're not like my uncle at all.'

He smiled. She looked at his broad shoulders. He now seemed big and comfortable and she suddenly felt overcome with fatigue.

She put her arms round his shoulder and curled up into his black sweater. Perhaps he was phoney, but she liked him. She could see that his face had changed. It was no longer condescending, but seemed very kind and warm.

'Is there a conflict in you?' he said.

'It's not a conflict in me. I feel there's a conflict in life – in psychology and religion.'

He began to laugh. Why was he laughing?

The phone rang and she picked it up.

'Hello, Andrea. I'm sorry to wake you up at this time of night.'

'It's all right.'

'Something's cropped up. It's Aunty Brenda – she's just gone into hospital. I hope it's not too serious – it's her kidneys as usual. Uncle Paul's come down from Leicester and he's got nowhere to stay. We can't put him up because we've got a houseful of guests. Do you know anyone who can put him up?'

Her mother's voice was very loud and Tim heard every word. She thought desperately and cupped her hand over the phone.

'Tim,' she whispered, 'would you be able to put my Uncle Paul up for the night at your place?'

'Of course,' he smiled in surprise.

'He can stay with a friend of mine,' she said to her mother. 'Where is he?'

'He's at the hospital. I'll give you the details. Does your friend have a car?'

'Yes.' She wrote down the address and put down the phone.

'How strange that it should happen tonight, just as I've been telling you all this.'

Tim laughed. 'Fate has had its revenge.'

She stared at him.

'Andrea, you thought I was phoney and I thought you were a smug little girl. You labelled me just as much as you thought I was labelling other people.'

She nodded and suddenly felt frightened. He looked at her, large eyes gleaming but remote. She realised that she was drawn to him and that he felt quite detached from her.

'I'm glad you've opened up about that old fear,' he said. 'You mustn't keep things bottled up in you. Bring it all out into the open.'

She handed him the piece of paper with the hospital details, and her hand was trembling.

'What are you afraid of?'

She turned away. She was afraid of Tim, because she

now knew that she was attracted to him and yet his interest in her was purely clinical. It was the interest of a psychologist and it hurt her.

She opened the door for him.

'You will come to the group next week, won't you?'

'Yes.'

He stood at the door, his figure framed against the blackness of the night beyond, staring at her. He had won. She felt overpowered. Is was as though the weight of all those bodied were crushing her, just as they had crushed Maureen.

He hesitated, as though reluctant to go, sensing that something was wrong and she knew that she could arouse his interest by displaying her hurt, but it was alien to the way she acted. She never played with people.

She smiled. 'It's very kind of you to go to this trouble for me.'

'That's all right.'

'Goodbye.'

She could sense her feelings being pulled to and fro. She felt she had lost her former boxlike compact sense of herself. She no longer existed according to what was good and instructive. The change was subtle, yet deep and drastic.

She closed the door shut after him. It was a sharp click as the hinges moved back into position, the sound of metal against wood.

She knew that there was now a conflict in her life between ideals and success and there was a conflict in herself between her former sense of security and serenity and her new self-distrust, and as she unplugged the electric fire and the lamps, and the lights went out, one by one, the room turned to darkness.

14   The Messenger

'MAEVE'S IN one of her acid moods today.'
Connie snapped out the sentence angrily, placing the card in the wrong compartment of the filing-cabinet.

'I suppose I'm not used to working for a boss so much younger than me. Goodness, she's the same age as my younger daughter and I wouldn't put up with any of that nonsense from her, I can tell you.'

Connie fastened the lowest button of her yellow cardigan and pulled it down over her plump hips.

'Still, I'm earning good money, so why grumble?'

Ben, the other filing clerk, who was never accustomed to speaking much, had nodded silently throughout this outburst.

The silence in the office was broken only by the rhythmic shuffling of the punch-cards they were filing. They each worked at a different rate so that the effect resembled a new type of musical instrument being played by amateurs with no sense of harmony.

The door burst open suddenly and Maeve walked in. She was pinning up a strand of blonde hair that had accidentally loosened as she walked along the corridor.

'God, that man – he drives me round the bend.'

'Which one?' asked Connie.

'Alfie, the messenger in Registry B. He gets all my letters muddled. Honestly, I don't know what this place is coming to and everybody just stands by and muddles on. Well, I'm not going to let him get away with it. I'm going to complain.'

She walked angrily out of the office, her high heels clattering on the lino floor. She was a short, plump woman with very pale skin and very blonde hair. She always reminded Connie of a well-scrubbed baby who had been put in charge of an office by mistake.

'Poor Alfie, she'll probably get him the sack and you know what—'

'Sshhh – she's coming back again.'

The door opened and Maeve collapsed into her chair. 'The whole postal system's up the creek,' she sighed, 'but Mr Wiley won't be back until tomorrow, so I'll go and see him about it then.'

The phone rang and Maeve picked it up, inspecting her nails at the same time. They were varnished a very dark red and shone out against her fingers like rose petals darkened in the heat of summer.

'It's not fair – such a nasty character to be as pretty as that,' Connie muttered to Ben. 'And you would think butter wouldn't melt in her mouth.'

'Sshhh.' Ben pointed to the phone. 'Something's up.'

Maeve was holding the phone between her shaking fingers. 'I'll be there as soon as I can.'

She put down the phone and stared into space, her blue eyes open and frightened.

'Is everything all right,' asked Connie.

'No, it's my husband. He's … he's been involved in some protest march and he's just been taken off to prison.'

They stared at her in amazement.

'I didn't bloody want him to get involved in bloody politics. It's not fair on me. I've got my career to think of and I worked hard enough for it.'

She looked coolly round the room and they followed her gaze. The office was immaculately tidy. There was not a form or a letter out of place, The furniture was carefully arranged. The telephone pads and telex messages were stacked in neat piles.

'I'm sure she has worked hard,' Connie whispered to Barry.

Maeve looked up in annoyance. 'I do hate all this whispering. It gets on my nerves.'

Connie winced and stepped back slightly. Maeve kicked the wastepaper bin out of her way with her left foot and put on her coat.

'Ben, you'd better come with me. I'd like to have an escort. I haven't been to a prison before.'

Ben flushed and put on his jacket awkwardly.

'He's not exactly a man yet, but he'll give me some support. How old are you, Ben?'

'Seventeen.'

'Yes, I thought so. Come on then.'

She flung the door open and marched briskly out of the office with Ben trailing behind her. They ran down the steps, down the road into the main street and along to the prison. The sun was shining brightly, but Ben felt a sense of apprehension. Maeve was running at full speed, panting for breath.

As they turned into the side road leading to the prison, they found a long queue of men standing at the gates with several shouting angrily. Some of them were drunk.

'They're all his comrades on that bloody march,' she whispered to Ben at the corner of the street.

He nodded and drew back, frightened.

'Well, don't just cower in the corner. You're supposed to be supporting me, not hiding under Mummy's skirt for protection.'

Ben moved a step forward and stood quivering with fright. Some of the men were carrying flick-knives. Many of them were dabbing at cuts and wounds with handkerchiefs. A nurse was rushing around giving medical aid. Policemen were blowing whistles and an ambulance was in the background, but despite all these semblances of law and order, the crowd was out of control. There were screams and groans and some of the men were brawled and punching each other.

'Please let me get through!' shouted Maeve. 'I've come to see my husband, Donald Smithson.'

'Are you his missus?' bellowed a bearded man with a banner in his hands. 'It's all his fault we had the police onto us. He started the trouble.'

'Yes, it was his fault,' came a chorus of voices.

'Let me bloody well get him,' Maeve screamed. 'Ben, help me. Don't just stand there like a gormless idiot. Help me.'

Ben stared at her. The bearded man approached and held an open flick-knife to his throat.

'What's your name, lover boy? What are you doing with Donald's missus, eh? Tell us that.'

'Nothing,' screamed Ben, though his voice came out like a high squeak. 'Nothing,' he repeated.

He turned round and ran back down the road, with one guilty look back at Maeve, who was left standing in the middle of the road.

'It's her gov'ner that started all this trouble,' someone shouted.

'Help! Help!' screamed Maeve.

She looked around desperately and suddenly on the other side of the road she saw Alfie, the messenger from the post-room, ambling slowly up the road with some parcels under his arm.

'Alfie, please save me!' she screamed. 'Help me! Come and save my life!'

There was an immediate babble of laughter.

'She thinks we're going to do her in,' laughed one man. 'Look at her. Terrified out of her wits. Never seen such a white face.'

'Alfie! Alfie!' she screamed.

He looked up and ambled across the road.

'Hello, Alfie,' came a chorus of shouts.

'Hello, Dad,' said the bearded man.

'Hello, Pete. You been up to something again?'

There was a loud burst of laughter.

'That's the understatement of the year. Did you hear that? He's a real comedian is old Alfie.'

'Are you all right, Mrs Smithson?'

'No, I'm not! Get me away from this place!'

'Never you worry. I'll help you back home. You leave the lady alone,' he shouted at the crowd of men. 'She's a respectable young lady.'

He took her by the arm and led her down the road. Just as they were nearing the office, they crossed the main road. Crossing in front of them were two police-man with a group of men. When they reached the pavement they shook the men by the hand and walked away from them back towards the prison. The man on the left turned round.

'Maeve!' he exclaimed.

'Donald! You bloody, bloody fool. Why did you get mixed up in all that rubbish.'

'It's all right, darling. We've all been released. There's been some mistake.'

'I'll say there's been some mistake. I nearly had my throat cut trying to find you. How many times have I told you to keep out of politics.'

'It wasn't my fault.'

'It never is. Well, you're not getting any dinner to-night, I can tell you. You can eat in a restaurant or with some of your marvellous friends – such good friends that you nearly get landed in gaol.'

She flung back her head and walked swiftly away to the office where she found Connie sitting open-mouthed at her desk, staring at Ben, who was hunched up in his chair, head in hand, sobbing.

'Bloody fool, you are,' said Maeve. 'You deserve the sack, though I suppose your filing's competent.'

She stood up and smoothed down her hair. 'Now what was I doing? Oh yes, I was preparing the report for the committee meeting next week.'

She picked up her fountain pen and a notebook and began to write. After a few minutes there was a knock on the door.

'Come in.'

A tall man in a black suit entered.

'Oh, Mr Wiley, I thought you wouldn't be back until tomorrow.'

'My conference finished early today, Mrs Smithson.' He leered at her. 'And very charming you look today, I must say.'

'Do you think so? Oh, I'm always in such a hurry, I never have time to make myself look remotely presentable.'

Her voice had assumed a slightly flirtatious tone. He pulled up a chair and smiled at her again.

'Not only do you always look charming, Mrs Smithson, but I must tell you that we have been highly praised about the work of this department – very high indeed.'

'Oh, thank you, Mr Wiley.'

'Since you were appointed to this role last year, we've managed to weed out all the inefficiency and slipshod work, I'm pleased to say.'

'Oh that reminds me,' said Maeve. 'I'm dissatisfied with Alfie's work. You know, the messenger in Registry B. I've had a great many complaints about him.'

'I don't think I'm acquainted with him.'

'You probably wouldn't recognise him.'

She laughed, her baby-blue eyes sparkling with mischief. 'He's an aged nonentity with spectacles and a bald head.'

'Oh, that one. Touché.'

'So I feel that perhaps something ought to be done …' She hesitated deliberately.

'Of course, of course, Mrs Smithson. We'll have to

find a replacement.'

He leaned back and looked at her appreciatively. 'It's a pleasure to find a beautiful woman running all this office machinery so efficiently, Mrs Smithson. It's nice to know that a few people manage to overcome the demands of bureaucracy and still retain the true essence of their femininity.'

She smiled and a dimple appeared on each cheek.

15   The Waiting

CELIA STOOD on the embankment, leaning out over the railings and gazed at the Thames. It was moving slightly, a drugged heaving of the upper layers of water and a lethargic swelling of the liquid below. Thick, grey and oily, like streaks of paint on canvas, but less selected. The liquid and semi-liquid sediments moved and alternated.

Celia felt that if she stared at it hard enough she would discover the knot of her inner world. Why had Philip labelled her a mirror? He had stared at her full in the face and said, 'You're not a person at all. You're a mirror. You simply reflect what you hear and what you see, and each time your surroundings change, you change. I can't live with a mirror.'

Celia had laughed and walked up to the glass-table in the corner of the dining-room. 'You sound like something out of Terence Rattigan.'

'Feeble jokes don't make any difference. You're never the same, Celia. I can't bear any inconsistency.'

It was true. During the six months that they had been living together she had been constantly changing, but it was a deliberate change. Philip had been taken in. She used to alter her mood and her ideas according to her clothes. It was a childish affectation and Philip was a fool to be so naïve. She blinked. Perhaps he was not naïve. Perhaps it was simply a polite excuse for leaving her.

She looked over the railings. The cold iron bars dug

119

into her neck. She felt mirror-like at that moment. There was no past, no future. Just her body, leaning over the railings and her eyes. If she could paint this scene, she would use vivid reds, greens, blues, blacks and whites in tiny speckles, so that from a distance it would look brown. But nothing ever looked straightforward to Celia. Philip had told her that her vision was 'microscopic'.

'You see tiny fragmented details. And that prevents you from seeing the real thing.'

'Not microscopic,' she had retorted. 'Microcosmic. Everything is reflected within the fragment.'

And even now, as she focussed her eyes on a streak of olive-green sludge, there was no solitude. She felt overwhelmed with visual sensation and her mind was buzzing with a kaleidoscope of ideas. The wind blew flat against her face and she gasped for breath. She turned around and ran across to the Embankment gardens.

She stopped short, as she recognised a woman seated on the bench by the fountains, feeding the pigeons. The woman was in her fifties, tall and angular, with straight black hair. As she turned to the left to pick up some crumbs, Celia recognised the brown skin and the arched eyebrows. They were Sarah's eyebrows. But Sarah probably looked quite, quite different now from her mother. Sarah had looked like that in her teens, at school, and in the first years of university: quiet and dark with straggly hair and gleaming Moroccan eyes, inherited from her Moroccan mother, just as she had inherited a taste for the unusual – flying saucers, Buddhism, entomology.

Many people thought these were affectations in Sarah, but not Celia, for she had met her mother. Sarah would spend hours pacing the country lanes, looking at the sky hopefully for meteorites, and when they did not turn up, she would retreat into her books. She would sit very still, like a small child, and the tiny iron ornament that hung on a chain around her neck would glint slightly, a splinter of gold upon black, and when she met strangers, she would talk very quickly, but Celia knew that this was not her real self – or was it?

One Saturday morning Celia had gone round to Sarah's house to lend her a book. Her mother was chopping up carrots in the kitchen. It was a large room, half-empty, with only the barest of necessities; a broom stood upside down against the pantry door.

Her mother sliced the carrots with quick movements. There was a long pause between each chop, despite their briskness: *chop … chop … chop … chop … chop.* The wooden board bounced up rhythmically after each attack.

Sarah was on her knees, scrubbing the floor. She looked up.

'Mother's so tired. I'm just giving her a hand.'

'Can I help?'

'No, you're a guest.'

And Celia had stood quietly in the doorway, watching the two dark figures chopping and scrubbing. There was an austerity about the room, which made her feel as though she had been cleansed with lemon-juice and then plunged into a bath of very cold water. The older woman paused and stretched open her palm.

'Bother! That knife has left a white mark right over my lifeline.'

'Now you won't be able to tell your own fortune, Mother.'

'Can you tell fortunes?' asked Celia.

The woman shook her head. 'I haven't done that for a long time.'

Her black hair rustled against her orange cotton blouse. Her neck shone brown against it like the bark of a banana tree.

Celia shifted onto the other foot. Sarah had finished scrubbing and wrung out the cloth in the sink. 'Let's go down to the museum,' she said, turning to Celia.

The two girls walked into the hall. As they opened the front door, Sarah's mother emerged from the kitchen. In the gloom of the hall her skin now seemed pale against her hair.

'I'll tell you one thing though, Celia,' she said. 'Everything comes to her who waits.'

Sarah laughed her strange, chortling laugh. 'What does that mean, Mother?'

'I waited until I was twenty-seven before I met your father. And then he suddenly popped up. I never gave up waiting.'

Celia blinked from her memories and looked up at the pigeons. The woman was bending over them. She was older now, and heavier, but the movements of her hair, as she threw the crumbs to the birds, were familiar: quick movements with a long pause between each.

Sarah had changed inevitably, but Celia had not. That was the curious thing about Celia: she simply mirrored everything around her, but she remained untouched by it. Inside she was still a little girl.

The last time Celia had seen Sarah was at a party, before she left England to emigrate to Australia. Sarah was wearing a red dress with lots of jewellery. She was laughing and talking a lot, and Celia had suddenly felt afraid of her – or perhaps it was not so much fear as envy of her gaiety and energy, for she herself was still an observer, passive and empty.

Philip was not the only person who had charged her with this defect, but his departure had hurt her more than anything else that had happened to her in her life. It was yet another notch on the totem pole of her failures and, as if it were the hundredth, it seemed conclusive. As he opened the front door of their flat, he had tripped over a case and smiled kindly.

'I'm sorry, but it's time you grew up.'

Celia had heaped together into a trunk her easel and paints, her books and papers, her guitar and perfumes and clothes and pottery. She had arranged them into neat piles and locked the trunk.

She had now been living in a bedsitter for two weeks. Only two weeks, but it had given her time to think. The trouble was that she was not a thinking person. She simply felt and reacted. Today, when she had been walking around London, she had tried to gather together the threads of her failures, to knot them together and to find the essence of her own true self, but it had eluded her. Perhaps what Philip said was true. Perhaps she was a parasite on other people and sponged up their blood to feed her own vitality.

The woman turned round and Celia hid behind a tree. She did not want to be seen. The woman, as if sensing that someone was there, picked up her bags and walked stiffly away across the grass. Celia walked up to the bench and sat down. Something jammed into her thigh and she jumped up quickly. It was a small grey and brown striped shopping bag. She had not noticed it. She picked it up and guiltily, against her own inclinations, opened it.

Inside were two sandwiches, a make-up case, and a book: the collected poems of William Blake. She opened the book and a photograph fell out into her lap. Turning it face upwards she saw the head of a small boy, with dark Moroccan eyes and arched eyebrows. The features seemed to pass from generation to generation, unaltered.

Sarah was a normal woman, who developed and changed and reproduced, while Celia herself was trapped by her reflectiveness. Her own character, her sense of being a real person, only emerged occasionally in a poem, a painting, a song. A moment of insight.

It began to rain. Sarah looked up at the grey sky and let the water trickle down her cheeks. Philip was gone and the years would pass her by. Yet she felt at peace. The rain fell down in quick-slow shafts, like the chopping of carrots.

Everything comes to her who waits.

16   A Chateau in Summer

MARY PICKED up the receiver.
'Hello.'
'It's Jennifer.'
'Who? I'm sorry?'
'Jennifer. I'm sure you must have forgotten me after all these years. We worked together with the refugee children ten years ago.'
'Yes of course I remember.'
'I found your phone number in the directory. Are you still teaching?'
'Yes. What made you suddenly remember me?'
'I was looking through a photograph album and found that ghastly photo of you bathing in the duck-pond with Solomon and Thérèse.'
Mary laughed.
'I'm giving a coffee party next month. On the tenth. Could you make it? I'll drop you an invitation. *Must dash.* Goodbye.'
The phone clicked and Mary stood in amazement, listening to the silence. She walked up to the mirror and stared at her reflection, fat and squat like a raspberry blancmange. She turned away in disgust and opened the french windows.
The bright sky dazzled her as she tried to recall Jennifer's face, but she could only visualise one feature at a time: large eyes, and then her long shoulders covered in the fingers of a child demanding a piggy-back. The tiny

bitten fingernails dug into her, grey against her white blouse. Finally she recalled the strip of orange-peel, which Jennifer would place in her mouth every lunchtime to amuse the children, while she was dishing out the food. One day it fell into her plate of cous-cous by mistake and the children had giggled hysterically.

The holiday home for refugee children had been set up in a chateau fifty kilometres from Paris just after the Algerian war. The children were frightened and homesick. Solomon, the supervisor, used to call them *petits sauvages*.

Mary remembered one night when she had been awoken by the screams of five-year-old Dominique, who was clapping her hands against her eyes, as if to obliterate the figures in her nightmare. The girl jumped out of bed and began to tear off the sheets. It took ten minutes for all the helpers at the chateau to calm her back to sleep.

Mary and Jennifer had been flown over from England by a refugee organisation. They were each in charge of five children and worked in conjunction with Pierre and Thérèse, who were due to study philosophy at the Sorbonne. All the helpers were in their late teens and had volunteered to work there in the summer gap between school and university.

Because they were understaffed, they rushed through their daily routine, which was crammed with activity, except for the afternoon siesta, when the monitors would sit down at the end of the long dormitory, watching the rows of sleeping children.

Mary recalled one such afternoon siesta on a Sunday

in July. The heat had blistered the paint on the window-sills. Jennifer was sprawled on a chair, dabbing her face with cologne, while Pierre was sitting on a window-sill, chewing grapes. He spat out the seeds into the palm of his hand and whispered to Jennifer as he chewed. Mary noticed, from the corner of her eye, the damp, woody fragments that sank into the flash of his hand as he spoke.

Opposite them sat Thérèse, gripping a large basket of peaches between her knees and reading aloud from a paperback called *L'homme inconnu* by Alexis Carrel, The front cover depicted the head of a man, and an identical image was superimposed across it like a dual exposure.

'What does this mean?' she asked Mary, but Mary was staring at Pierre, fascinated by his eyes. He was heavy and thickset in build, with an almost phlegmatic, placid countenance, but his eyes were narrow and black, and flickered to and fro continually.

Thérèse prodded Mary again. 'What does this mean?' she repeated. '"A man can only know himself through his parents." That is ridiculous. I've never known my parents. I was brought up in a home like this one, but ten times worse.'

She scratched her head sharply at the recollection. She was short and stocky with brownish skin, dark features and jagged hair. Her eyebrows were thick and nearly met at the centre. Sometimes she looked almost repulsive. She moved clumsily and was always cursing when she tripped on a branch.

And yet the children would stare at her, enraptured, as she made mock-angry faces and then smiled in comic alternation. They would turn to her when they were homesick, and bury themselves in her baggy skirt; they adored her and would sit three at a time on her large lap, pulling at her jumper and asking questions.

She in return would be consistently kind to them, always patient and never out of temper. That morning she had spent four hours in the garden with the older boys and Mary noticed the streaks of perspiration and dirt that lined her cheeks.

'It is very difficult to understand,' she whispered again to Mary. 'The philosophy is complicated.'

Pierre pulled a peach out of her basket. Jennifer adored him and followed him around continually. She was always coming up with games and projects that would involve the two groups of children.

As much as Thérèse loved the children, with adults she could be vindictive and for some reason she had taken an immediate dislike to Jennifer, which was increased by the latter's obvious frivolousness. Thérèse would mock Jennifer's adoration for Pierre behind her back to Mary, who tended to listen to her in silence, as she herself was equally as bewildered by the intensity of Jennifer's love for Pierre as she was by Thérèse's venom, all the more so because Jennifer was always so kind and playful with the children.

As Jennifer giggled with Pierre, Thérèse whispered in Mary's ear, 'Look at her. The way she talks to Pierre all the time. She's behaving like a three-year-old. It's so childish.'

Mary pretended not to hear. A few minutes later, Jennifer ran out of the room to fetch her embroidery and Thérèse turned to Pierre.

'Don't waste so much time talking to that girl. She should pay more attention to the children. She is irresponsible.'

Jennifer walked in again, trailing a tablecloth beneath her elbow and flopped onto a chair.

'Pierre,' continued Thérèse, 'what does this mean. "If an unknown man comes to your door..."'

'You read too much.' he replied. 'It's better to think than to read, or better still, remember things you've learnt off by heart. For instance, the other week I was waiting for my train at Gare St Lazare and I was half an hour early, so I walked up and down the platform reciting from Corneille's *Le Cid*, and it was a wonderful feeling.'

'To yourself or aloud?' asked Jennifer.

'Aloud.'

Thérèse gave Mary a meaningful look.

Jennifer choked with laughter, burying her head in the tablecloth. 'They must have thought you were crazy,' she said.

Thérèse rubbed a bitten peach against her face and Mary noticed the pale patch, where the dust from her face had been wiped off and replaced by a fine layer of juice.

A child in the bed near them stirred, woke up, and started crying. Thérèse ran over to him and crouched down by his pillow.

'Sshhh,' whispered Thérèse, her tone becoming at once gentle; she soothed him down, talking quietly and gently to him.

When Mary looked up at the window, she saw Pierre in the garden carrying the bell from the shed. He swung it over his shoulder, holding it in place so that it would not ring as he walked.

Jennifer sat watching him, chewing the curled ends of her long hair, as she always did when she was worried.

'What's the matter?' asked Mary.

Jennifer paused, gazing at Pierre and anticipating the noise from the bell, screwed up her face and whispered to Mary, 'He doesn't like me.'

The bell broke into noisy peals and Mary ran towards the girl in the nearest bed and shook her awake, while Jennifer hovered by her side.

'What do you mean he doesn't like you?'

'I know he doesn't – I mean, he's indifferent to me – but he thinks you're an astute person.'

'Astute?' said Mary. 'What an odd thing to say.'

A little girl in the far corner of the dormitory began to wail and Jennifer rushed over. Crouching down she made funny faces at her, which soon made her giggle hysterically.

'Shhhh, Dominique.'

As the bell continued to clang, Solomon rushed into the room to announce the end of the siesta and the children began to shout and giggle. He was attacked by three small boys, who pretended to shoot him, pointing their fists and shrieking. Other children were throwing pillows and clothes at each other.

'That's enough,' Solomon shouted.

Three small girls pulled at the back of his shirt, and

he swivelled round in mock anger, ruffling their hair.

Later they took all the children into the garden for tea. Mary was handing round plates of bread, chocolate and oranges when Solomon walked over to her. He towered above her and pulled at his beard.

'Thérèse tells me that Jennifer is not taking her work seriously,' he said.

Mary sighed. The beard looked like a brush from below. She could see the gleam of light as he adjusted his spectacles nervously, and she realised that he was worried.

'I think that's just gossip,' she said.

They both looked across the garden to where Jennifer stood at the far end talking to Pierre and juggling with a long French breadstick between her hands.

Two triplets ran up to Mary and tugged at her skirt. 'Sing us a song. Please sing us a song,' they shouted.

Solomon was still gazing at Pierre and Jennifer. He relieved Mary of the plates of bread and chocolate and continued to pass them around, while she say on the grass with the group of children.

'Sing "Caroline était malade",' said one of them and Mary sang:

'Caroline était malade,
On l'emmène à l'hôpital,
L'hôpital était brulé,
Caroline était sauver.'

'Sing as another song, Mary. Sing "Petit Capitaine",' said one of the triplets.

'No, you sing it, Dominique.'

The little girl opened her mouth very wide and, pushing her fringe out of her eyes, began singing:

'Petit capitaine, revenant du guerre cherchent son amour.
Petit capitaine, revenant du guerre cherchent son amour.'

The song trickled out after a few minutes and turned into a dance. The children hopped up and down in a circle, gasping and pushing each other. Then Mary suddenly felt her right arm being pulled. The pressure was painful. She turned round and Jennifer was jerking her arm to and fro. She pulled it away.

'Have you see Chantal?' Jennifer whispered.

'No.'

Jennifer started to chew her hair in agitation and then pulled at it, shouting, 'Oh God, I'm supposed to be looking after her. Where the bloody hell is she?'

Chantal was the youngest child in Jennifer's group. She was only four and was particularly undisciplined, having a habit of wandering away out of sight.

'Oh hell and damnation,' Jennifer muttered. 'This is too much.'

Solomon had warned Jennifer that Chantal might try to run away. She ran frantically round the garden in long strides, crouching beneath bushes and trees and peeping through gaps in the fences, then ran back to Mary who was collecting up the plates and beakers and placing them on the trolley.

'Look, Mary, if she's run away, please, please, would you take the blame? Pierre will be furious with me.'

Mary looked at Jennifer in amazement as Solomon appeared at the back of the house, escorting three of the older boys. He walked angrily up to Jennifer, who prodded Mary sharply in the ribs.

'Where's Chantal? Why weren't you looking after her?'

Jennifer prodded Mary again.

'I was looking after her,' Mary blurted out, 'while Jennifer was playing with the triplets. She must have run down the alley.'

Solomon snapped his fingers in fury and shouted to Pierre, 'Keep an eye on the others, for goodness sake – every one of them. This is too much.'

They all ran down the alley, kicking loops of grass out of the way with their ankles. Halfway down they found Chantal's red jumper, with one of the sleeves soaked in pond-water. Solomon picked it up and frantically ran towards the woods beyond the garden.

'Each of you run in different directions!' he shouted. 'As fast as you can! Hurry up! Quickly!'

Mary climbed through the fence and made her way through the undergrowth; pieces of brittle soil flicked up onto her ankles and a cloud of dust from the dry soil billowed around her, making her cough.

'Chantal! Chantal!' she called as she approached a bed of nettles and then stopped in horror. The little girl was lying crumpled up on her back, motionless on the ground, next to the nettles. Her long black was tangled in the weeds behind her head, and her arms and legs were beginning to blister in swollen red patches from the stings.

Mary knelt in the nettles, oblivious of the pain in her ankles, and pulled Chantal out of the nettles and into a grassy patch nearby. She took her wrist, feeling for a pulse, but couldn't tell if there was one. The child flopped back, heavy and drooping, her arms dangling. As Mary knelt there staring at her in terror, the ferns and grasses seemed to rush in on her like a sickly dazzle of green. Mary shouted to Solomon, 'Come here – I've found her!'

Jennifer appeared around the corner and started to scream. The noise was curiously deep in tone, more like a groan than a scream, and seemed to vibrate against the ferns. The child's eyelids started to flicker and her mouth opened in surprise when she saw the two girls bending over her.

When Solomon joined them and Chantal suddenly realised that she was the object of their concern, she started to cry. It was not an unhappy sound but rather an effort to respond to the situation.

Solomon lifted her gently onto his shoulder and they hurried back into the garden. As Mary's hand brushed against the undergrowth, she felt again the giddiness that had crushed her into the greenness. The motionless child had seemed grotesque, like a mammoth spider.

What would she have done if Chantal had been hurt? Would she have taken the blame for Jennifer? She simply did not know and now it seemed that the question was irrelevant. They reached the house where Thérèse treated Chantal's arms with a layer of ointment.

In the garden the group of children had shaped itself into a crescent. Jennifer and Pierre were sitting in the middle of a large group of children and Jennifer had her hands on her head and was making one of her funny faces. The two little ones once again tugged at Mary's skirt.

'Sing another song! We want to hear a song!'

The sun was setting and shadows appeared across the lawn. Pierre pulled out a tuft of grass and blew upon it, producing a harsh, vinegary squawk. The triplets covered their ears and began to wail. The other children in Mary's group wanted to imitate Pierre and pulled fistfuls of grass from the lawn, trying to blow.

As they blew the grass, pieces of dry earth fell off, like rotting wood. Laughter, buzzing, and strange, funny noises filled the air. Thérèse was crouching like a tent over two small girls who were pulling each other's hair. Solomon began playing a recorder in the corner of the garden and a circle of children gathered round him. They started to dance, hopping up and down and shouting, until they all tripped over one another and fell into a heap.

Jennifer and Mary began to sing and the haunting notes of the folk song seemed to beckon and induce the twilight over the darkening garden.

Jennifer whispered in Mary's ear: 'Pierre says I'm an unusual person.' She smiled with pride and stretching herself out on the grass, rolled over and over. Some of the children imitated her, and as Mary watched the rows of rolling bodies in the shadows, she shivered as a sudden apprehension of death seized her.

The telephone rang again. She blinked and turned away from the french window.

'Hello.'

'Hello, it's Jennifer again. Look, I know this must sound ridiculous after I've just invited you, but I'm calling off the coffee party.'

'Calling it off?'

'Yes, I've just had a telegram from my husband in Switzerland and he wants me to join him out there for a couple of months. I'm sure you'll remember him – Solomon – he was the supervisor at the chateau we worked at.'

'Solomon? But I thought it was Pierre—'

'Solly's involved in some trade conference and he thinks I can help him. I can't imagine how. Anyway, it's such a pity about the coffee party. We'll have to have a get-together some time, when I get back.

'Yes, that would be nice.'

'OK, I'll be seeing you then. Bye.'

Mary replaced the receiver. Jennifer was so impulsive. She was sure that she would never see her again. The phone-call had just been an impulse. The room suddenly felt empty and cold.

She walked over to the window. The sun was setting in a pink blur against the chimneys of the houses opposite, and in the garden next door she could hear the expressive, infinitely joyful, infinitely sad sound of children squabbling and shrieking.

17 I Never Knew His Name

MY SISTER had asked me to babysit that Wednesday because she and her husband wanted to go to a viola concert at the Wigmore Hall. I opened the front door with the spare key and made my way into the empty living room. I was starting to tidy up when I heard a scuffle in the next room, which was the kitchen, and then a face appeared at the open hatch between the two rooms: a small, male head with sandy hair, narrow blue eyes and thin features.

'Don't get a shock,' he said. 'Beryl and I have just been discussing a painting she'd like to buy.'

He held up a large green and brown landscape with a black river running between rows of trees.

'Is she going to buy it?' I asked.

'She couldn't afford it. It's five pounds.'

'I laughed. 'A fortune. I rather like it actually.'

I peered at it closely. The green trees stood out almost three-dimensionally from the grey sky.

'It's a new technique,' he said. 'I've spent three years finding the right way of mixing the colours to get the right contrast.'

'I'll buy it,' I said. 'Beryl's always been rather miserly. I'd like to have that hanging up in my bedroom.'

He nodded, and handed me the painting through the hatch.

'I hope I didn't give you a fright,' he said. 'I stayed on after Beryl left to listen to the news.'

He pottered around in the kitchen, kicking a piece of newspaper out of the rug with his shoe. I didn't quite trust him. I believed his story as to why he was there and the picture, but I felt that there was something odd about his deprecating laugh. Nevertheless I handed over a five pound note in silence and began to cough.

'I've got to go,' he said. 'Some people to see about a new batch of watercolours.'

He buttoned up his sports jacket and I felt once again an incongruity in his apparent status as an artist and the suburban neatness of his collar and tie. I closed the door behind him and heard the sound of his footsteps clattering down the road.

It was a bright summer evening and there was nothing worth watching on television, so I sat on the verandah and opened a book of reproductions of paintings of the 1930s. The evening light shone down pinkly upon the glossy pages – a windmill with a farmyard in the background. The brown shadows stood out curiously, three-dimensionally. I looked down at my picture and noticed the same texture of dots and shade.

I turned over the next few pages and found to my surprise a series of similar paintings. Finally, on the second to last page there was a reproduction of the painting I had just bought.

My mouth fell open in astonishment and my heart began to pound. It was an uncomfortable feeling. Were my eyes playing tricks on me? I looked again. In the corner of the reproduction was the signature, '*John Vandals*'.

There was no signature on my painting. I looked at it

closely. The trees in the left-had corner were at a different angle to the Vandals reproduction. I had bought a forgery. I suddenly realised with horror that the man I had been speaking to had not been talking to Beryl at all, but had somehow let himself into the house.

I walked quickly into the kitchen. The door was unlocked and on the doorstep there were pieces of newspaper.

Who had I been talking to: a forger, the artist himself, or a dealer in stolen goods?

I never discovered, but whenever I see the trees jutting out of the evening gloom I experience that same sense of incongruity, of something slightly amiss.

18 Bureaucracy

W HEN GILLIAN was offered her post of Head of the Records Department she felt flattered at being given a promotion and began to organise her life around the one aim of maximum efficiency. Chalmers & Co. were known to the general public as the makers of fine woollen sweaters, but to Gillian they simply represented security.

She responded to the large organisation of the office like a bee to a hive, returning to it each morning with a sense of diligence and propriety. She began to work in her tea-breaks and lunch hour and often took casefuls of files home in the evening to check.

As the months passed by, her office reputation grew, and her circle of personal friends dwindled. In the end the only person she saw regularly was Richard, who had been going out with her for two years and found it hard to break the habit, despite the increasing narrowness of their conversation.

One Friday lunchtime, when they were sitting in a pizza bar, he tried to explain to Gillian what he felt was wrong with her.

'You're not a human being any more. You've completely succumbed to bureaucracy.'

A look of boredom passed over her face. 'I've heard that one before.'

'And your lipstick's too bright. Don't you notice how you look any more?'

Gillian got up angrily from her chair. 'I don't mind insults about my job. They're rather boring, but I'm not putting up with personal insults.'

Richard nodded slowly. 'You can't face the truth.'

She placed her share of the lunch bill on the table and ran out of the restaurant. It was a sunny day and she had been feeling quite excited at the prospect of her holiday. That evening she was going to stay with her aunt in Essex for a fortnight. Richard's attitude to her was unfair. She ran down the street adroitly dodging groups of pedestrians. He was probably jealous.

When she reached the office she burst into tears at the thought of Richard's unkindness. Mrs Kaye, the personnel director, collided with her coming down the stairs.

'What's up, Gillian?'

'I've just had a row with my boyfriend.'

'Oh dear. Why don't you take the afternoon off? You've been working too hard. A few hours in the fresh air will cheer you up.'

Gillian grinned and collected her cases from the office. Twenty minutes later she was on the train to Colchester. It was late August and the soft air floated in through the window. Every time Gillian looked at the houses and gardens that flashed by, she felt tears welling.

By the time she reached her aunt's cottage in the countryside near Colchester it was six o'clock. The place was deserted and she conjectured that her aunt must be still in town, doing some shopping. To kill the time before her aunt returned, she decided to go for a walk. She selected a poetry book from a bookshelf in the cosy living room and began walking down the country lane bordering the cottage. The openness of the cornfield countryside soothed here and she started to feel that there was nothing to worry about.

She sat down on a grassy verge and read a few poems. All was peaceful, with the smell of grass, a distant humming and a warm, blue sky. The air seemed to be steamy, lifting her a little and then dropping her. She felt as though she were swimming. She got up and walked into the cornfield and lay down in it, burying her face in the corn. Suddenly a line of filing numbers disturbed her serenity, only to be replaced by Richard's thin lips and beard. As green turned to black she fell asleep.

She awoke with a thudding heart to find someone standing over her: a man in a white shirt with his sleeves rolled up to reveal bulging muscles on his forearms. His hair was grey and close-cropped. She screamed and ran back over the grass towards her aunt's cottage.

She ran into the bedroom and sank into a chair. Her head was muzzy and when she looked in the mirror she saw that her face was completely white. How foolish to be exposed on the grass like that. She gazed in the mirror. Richard was right. Her lipstick was too light and he was also right about her obsession with work.

She sat down in the armchair and gazed through the tiny windows across to the cornfields and wondered who the man was and whether he had intended to attack her when there was a knock on the door.

As she ran to open it, she suddenly realised that it couldn't be her aunt, who of course would have her own door-key. But by now it was too late and she screamed again as the man in the white shirt towered before her in the front porch.

'Sorry if I alarmed you, miss, but I think you dropped this.'

He handed her the book of poems and wandered off up the road.

She gazed after him and then looked down at the book. The page fell open at the last poem she had been reading before she fell asleep:

What is this life if, full of care,
We have no time to stand and stare?

She stood and stared after the man, and at that moment decided to slip out of the net of bureaucracy before it was too late.

19   The Summer School

RACHEL OPENED the door of the lecture hall and turning to Carole said, 'I do wish we didn't have so much free time on this course. I can't imagine what they expect us to do for five hours between lunch and dinner. Crowle is hardly a sightseers' Mecca.'

She pulled the skirt of her Paisley dress straight. The wrinkled cotton stretched for a moment and then sagged back into its old folds.

'Mind you, I'm glad of a rest from teaching. I get so exhausted talking non-stop all the time.'

Carole narrowed her eyes to prevent them from expressing her amusement.

'You're squinting slightly. Is the sun too hot for you? You're rather thin for your age. When I was twenty-four I was as plump as a duck with mulberry sauce.'

Carole laughed.

'I picked up a lot of odd expressions in Africa. I had to do something to while away the time so I used to swot up odd pieces of jargon.'

The two women were standing in the courtyard of Crowle Hall, a residential college for further education. The summer school on 'Culture and Religion in Asia and Africa' had attracted thirty-seven participants, most of them teachers and clergymen. Carole had welcome the week's holiday from her local government post. The others in the office had laughed when they heard the subject of the course.

'We'll have to mind our Ps and Qs when you get back,' Hilary, her supervisor, had remarked. 'No more loose talk and swearing. What on earth induced you to spend your precious leave time on that, Carole? You could have had a week on the Riviera, soaking in the glorious sunshine and thinking beautiful thoughts. You're an odd fish, you know.'

Carole saw her own reflection in the mirror as she stood with her left hand on the Xerox machine. She really did look like a fish – a plaice or a sole perhaps. She was wearing a dressed spotted with black polka dots and her face and limbs were colourless.

'I don't want to sunbathe. I want to take my mind off all this ...'

Hilary snorted. 'What you mean is you want to listen to a load of boring old lecturers so that you can take your mind off your broken heart. I've heard it all a hundred times before.'

She tapped her varnished nails against the varnished desk. A series of overlapping patters.

'By the time you get to my age – and I'm only forty-five – you won't care two hoots about all that. I suppose I'm hardened. it comes with age.'

Carole looked up from her daydreaming as Rachel tapped her on the shoulder.

'You see that elderly couple over there – Phoebe and Tommy. He's eighty-seven and she's sixty-six. I only hope I'm as sprightly as that when I'm eighty-seven. He was one of the pioneers of the Humanists movement, you know. He's a real old renegade. Swears like a trooper.'

'I know,' said Carole. 'They live a few miles down the road in one of the council flats.'

'Really.' Rachel's eyes focussed with interest. She pursed her lips shrewdly. 'I'd like to visit their flat. I'd like to see how they manage for themselves.'

She strode across the courtyard. Tommy and Phoebe could hear her coming.

'Care to go for a drive this afternoon?' Rachel asked them. 'We'd love to come and visit you.' She beckoned Carole to join them. 'Come on, it'll give us all something to do.'

Phoebe smiled expansively. 'I'd be glad if our humble abode would help to alleviate the general boredom.'

They walked across the road to Rachel's car.

'It's damned boring. Damned boring,' said Tommy. 'I don't know why I inflict education on myself. I should be past it at my age.'

They all climbed into Rachel's car.

'You've been very quiet, Carole,' said Tommy.

'She's busy helping to reorganise out local government system,' said Phoebe, 'aren't you dear? I used to be in local government too before Tommy and I started seeing each other two years ago.'

Carole looked surprised.

'Nobody believes us. We only got married last summer. Of course we've both been married before. And it's worked out so convenient. Now that we're living in Tommy's flat with both our furniture, it's proving much cheaper, much more convenient.'

'She only married me for my money,' Tommy quipped.

Phoebe patted his white head. 'Nonsense, dear. It was your dynamic, youthful outlook on life that attracted me.' She smiled indulgently. Despite her sixty-six years she had retained the pink and white look of a gigantic elf.

Carole giggled. She found Phoebe absurd but reassuring.

The car drove swiftly through the winding lanes. The trees on either side pressed down against the windows. Each time they swerved round a corner, Carole felt her stomach lurch and with the physical sickness came the blackness of the past few weeks. Always the same picture appeared vividly in her mind.

The day after their quarrel she had seen Phil standing at the tube station with a group of students, gangly arms and raucous laugh. And as she stepped onto the train she had stared at his features without him seeing her, and she had recognised for the first time that he was totally happy. He was not looking at anybody. He was simply laughing to himself and it was his self-sufficiency that hurt her, made her jealous.

Then as people began to press around her in the tube, the window was obscured and she felt part of the crowd of Londoners, locked unwillingly into each others' tentacles.

She felt a prod on her arm and the memories of Phil faded as Rachel's plump face intruded itself on her vision.

'This is Crowle Museum, Carole. Let's go and have a look at the specimens of local history.'

Carole stared out of the car, unwilling to enter the

whitewashed building with black windows. She walked around the main exhibit hall with the same curious aversion. Stuffed birds, pressed flowers, old fossils. There was something deathly about the slow trudge of their footsteps in the empty hall. A group of people were walking round the hall from the other side.

Tommy suddenly stood stock-still and wiped his forehead with a handkerchief.

'Got to get out of this place.'

'Are you ill?' Rachel went white with alarm.

He forced a cough. 'No, take a lot to make an old horse like me ill. I'm in what's called an embarrassing situation. My first wife's standing there by the door.'

They followed him as he walked quickly back to the car.

'I didn't realise your first wife was still alive,' said Rachel.

'Oh, that's quite all right. I've been divorced three times. But I'm not in the mood to face her recriminations. We had an almighty row before we finally broke up. Thirty years ago, that was.'

Phoebe laughed. 'I should be thankful for that squabble. Or else we'd never be in the happy state of matrimony we are today.'

They got back in the car, Rachel switched on the engine and they drove quickly away.

'Good Lord, right old bag she was,' said Tommy. 'Glad I saw the last of her.'

They all laughed.

'One thing about Tommy,' said Phoebe, 'he never gives in.'

'I know my own mind. I never give in.'

'And now let's go and have a nice cup of tea at our humble abode,' said Phoebe.

'I'd rather have a drop of rum,' said Tommy.

His voice quivered at the end. Carole caught sight of his face in the driving mirror.

He looked like a fish. White face and pale blue eyes. A drowned fish – a plaice or a sole.

20   A Wish

I T WAS only recently that Angela had become conscious of the way her personality had changed. This alteration had been gradual, and had speeded up in recent years. Perhaps the most important thing she had learnt in the last decade was the value of time. There seemed to be so much that she would like to do, and so little time left over from her nine to five-thirty job.

The answer seemed to her at first to be condensation. She would perform everything at the maximum speed. Thus she consumed meals in seven minutes, wrote two novels in six months, joined four clubs, various religions and organisations and undertook two weekly commitments.

After a short time this method proved to Angela and to everyone else to be totally unsuccessful. The result of pouring quantities of events into a short space of time was like a suitcase bulging with too many clothes. Each garment was squashed and mangled. The creases and smudges were indelible. She realised that nothing was finished, and the momentary enjoyment of variety and a Bohemian disorder soon evaporated.

Her next wish grew out of the perfectionist desire to live life to the full on a small but faultless scale. The clubs and evening classes were thinned out with the ruthlessness of a scientific gardener.

One hour spent in cleaning and polishing her flat seemed as feat of artistry. She would stare at the polished furniture and neat piles of books and feel an unaccustomed pity for her married friends, whose rooms were dishevelled with toys and baby clothes,

One Sunday afternoon she was playing with her cousin's two small children. Half-eaten bread and marmalade had slipped onto the carpet. A doll dressed in Swiss national costume with both arms missing lay by the fireguard. There was a large crack down the left side of its face.

Jeremy, aged three, ran up to the fireguard and tried banged the bread against it. There was a crash as his sister pulled the coffee table over and two glasses of orangeade seeped into the red carpet.

But then as she watched the scarlet wool gradually lightening to ginger, she realised that change and disorder were part of the natural state of affairs.

21   The Record

ANNA STOPPED dancing and flopped into the sofa breathlessly.

'We've run out of dance records,' shouted Ken to the assembled guests in the darkened room.

'Put on some folk,' giggled a voice. 'There's some in the cupboard, under the box of dominoes.'

Ken rummaged in the cupboard and placed a pile of records on the record player.

Anna snuggled up into the corner of the sofa and placed two cushions under her head. She fell into a doze as the record started playing.

'It's not really folk, but it will do,' said Ken.

Anna was listening to the guitar, that seemed to store the darkness in strips of sound.

'But now they only block the sun
They rain and snow on everyone ...'

She was taken back to a cold winter in her adolescence. She buried herself deeper in the cushions and cast her mind back. She had been staying in a large old house in Sussex. It had snowed for three weeks solidly. Every day she would leap out of bed hopefully, to see whether it had melted, but always the same cold carpet of whiteness covered the surrounding gardens and fields.

The house belonged to her uncle and aunt, but they

were travelling on the continent and meanwhile the house was occupied by her cousins Kathy and Nicky,

For the first few weeks they all got on pleasantly together. Kathy and Anna spent most of the day reading and studying in front of the fire, but Nicky began to grown argumentative.

'He's recovering from a broken heart,' Kathy told Anna nonchalantly. She was fond of reducing emotions to a manageable formula. 'His girlfriend Stephanie left him last month and she's got engaged to another bloke.'

'Oh.' Anna did not enjoy gossip. She stared at the fire in the living room and continued to read. It was a large, bare room with an orange-red carpet and brown curtains. A huge coal-fire dominated the room.

One Monday afternoon the two girls were drinking tea, when Nicky rushed in and turned the radio on the sideboard up to full volume.

'That's Stephanie singing,' he said.

'It can't be,' said Kathy scornfully.

'It is, I recognise her voice.'

'Oh, Nicky, don't be such a sentimental old goose. Can't you just grow up and forget about Stephanie?'

He looked at her for a long time, His face was white and his eyes were squinting like small black stones. He turned abruptly and ran out of the house.

Kathy lay back in her chair and drummed her fingers against the arm of the chair. The room felt very cold. Draughts were blowing through gaps in the windows and under the door.

'You shouldn't have upset Nicky,' said Anna.

'It's not fair. Just because you are two years older

than him, you still treat him like a little boy.'

'He'll always be my younger brother, however old he is.'

Kathy flicked back her hair. It hung behind her back in black rats tails.

'God, I feel a real mess today,' she continued. 'Let's go for a walk. I need the exercise.'

The two girls put on their coats and began to make their way through the powdery snow. They walked in silence, both absorbed in their own thoughts.

'God, we'll go blind from this dazzle. I can't stand it much longer,' said Kathy.

'Let's just go as far as Macey's farm and then we can turn back,' suggested Anna.

The walk turned into a run and as they ran faster Anna looked up and realised that it had started to rain. They ran on past the old farm shacks and the two wishing wells until they came to the entrance of Macey's farm and then stopped short.

Two ambulance-men were lifting Nicky's body from the snow which was quickly turning to slush beneath the pelting rain, while nearby the driver of the car that had knocked him over was being questioned by the police...

'Funny,' said Ken, as Anna opened her eyes, it's a Joni Mitchell song but it's not Joni singing. I don't recognise the singer and there's nothing on the label. I wonder who it is?

'*I've looked at clouds from both sides now.*'

'I know her first name,' Anna said as if still trapped somewhere between past and present. 'It's Stephanie.'

22   The Sky

T WAS 5.25 on a Thursday afternoon. Beams of sunlight shone onto the desks in the office where the two girls were tidying their letters, invoices and envelopes.

Abbie was tired. She was looking forward to the boat trip with Graham tonight. She would have to hurry to catch the bus down to the river, and she hadn't even bought the tickets yet. She had promised to pay for the tickets, because Graham was still studying and by Thursday he was always short of money.

As she fitted the envelopes into the wire-tray, she looked out of the window. White clouds, moving so gently that it made her giddy to stare at them. She always felt strange when she looked at the sky. Its blue and white patches seemed to mock the grey shabbiness of the office.

She looked up again. The dazzle of eggshells against a Wedgwood plate. She felt that the sky was happy to communicate something to her. It was fanciful, even magical, but the more she looked out of the window, the more she felt that the blue expanse was vibrating and stretching.

'What are you looking at?' Diane asked from the other end of the office.

'The sky. I feel as though it's talking to me.'

Diane swung around quickly and her large lips smiled between strands of red hair. 'There's an old man up there with a white beard and he's looking down and saying, "Abbie, have you been a good girl today? Have you done your good deed for the day?"'

Abbie laughed.

Diane looked out of the window and sighed. 'When I look at the sky I just feel terrible lonely, as though I were on a tiny boat in the middle of a huge ocean and I feel alienated and frightened. I suppose you think my fears are affectations.'

'No, I don't.'

'John does. He gets furious with me. He says it's all a pose of pseudo-sensitivity. It's ghastly being married to a psychologist. One can't get away with anything.'

Abbie put on her coat and scarf.

'What a pretty scarf,' said Diana. 'Where did you get it?'

'In that boutique just next to the deli.'

Diane sat down and groaned again. 'Oh dear, it's such a damned nuisance. I'm going to a party late to-night. It starts at about eleven o'clock and I saw the most beautiful outfit in that boutique for a very reasonable price. It was a dress and jacket in emerald green with coffee-coloured patterns all over it. And it would just go with my hair. But John was too bloody stingy to give me the money for it. He said I'd have to pay for it myself, and I've spent nearly all my paypacket.'

'I'll lend it to you,' said Abbie impulsively. She opened her bag and handed Diane the money.

'Oh, you are super. Now you've done your deed for the day.'

'I must hurry. I've got to catch the bus,' said Abbie.

She ran out of the office, through the crowded street

as far as the bus stop. It was a clear July afternoon. There was a long queue of twenty or so people in front of her. She opened her bag automatically to check on her money and gasped when she found that her purse was empty.

She stared at a pony and cart trotting down the dusty road in the heat. She had overestimated the remainder of her own paypacket. An elbow prodded her in the back and she moved forwards jerkily, treading on the foot of a woman in front.

'I'm sorry.'

She had arranged to meet Graham in Greenwich. Panic seized her. No money left to meet him. No boat-trip down the river. She couldn't even ring him, because he could be anywhere at this time of day. Her heart beat loudly. The loud throb pressed against her eardrums, together with the sound of sparrows, newspaper sellers, giggling schoolgirls and a crying toddler.

Where had all the money gone? A series of images flashed before her eyes – newspapers, paperbacks, underwear, meals, drinks, bus tickets, two new blouses, an electricity bill. Of course, she had completely forgotten about the electricity bill. No wonder her purse was empty. There was nothing to be done but to walk back to her flat, but she decided against this: it was too hot to stay indoors. She wanted to be out in the open air.

She made her way across the street to the Embankment and walked several miles along the edge of the river. After some time the pedestrians thinned out and soon the street was practically deserted. The sun was setting and she could feel the coolness of the river. As the heat had worn off, so had the sense of her own ineptitude.

She looked up at the sky. It was no longer cornflower blue but a pale, watery grey and the clouds were wispy. The sky looked less inviting. She felt that it was no longer trying to communicate with her and as this thought struck her, she shrugged her shoulders, as though a weight of conscience had rolled off her back.

She continued to walk speedily, her legs sturdy and energetic but her mind empty; yet it was not a dull vacancy but rather a placid release as though she were discarding her thoughts one by one with every step she took.

Across the river she could see wharves and old office blocks. They loomed black and dark grey in the evening air. It began to rain very lightly and drops clung to her cheeks and hair. It seemed as though she were unable to stop walking or even to change her direction and turn back or cross the road away from the river.

She was impelled to follow the tidal flow of the Thames, and as she moved forward, she felt that she was somehow being unified and submerged within the river, its grey-green waters had become part of her.

Memories of her childhood floated before her as she walked. She had a vivid recollection of her mother tugging her along by the hand on a hot summer evening, when she was five.

'Hurry up, Abbie,' her mother had said. 'Don't dawdle, staring at the river the whole time. We haven't come out here for the walk, you know. We've got to get back home as quickly as possible.'

Abbie laughed. She stretched her arms and circled them in the air. Her mother was far away and she could dawdle as much as she liked.

It began to rain properly. She looked at her watch. it was 10.30. In the distance she could see the lights of a riverside pub. She returned to reality. She would have to make the long trek back home again. It would take several hours, but even now she did not mind. She was still alert and energetic. She decided to take a peep at the pub and then make her way back home again as quickly as possible.

She walked to the entrance of the pub and stared in amazement. A party seemed to be taking place in the garden. The bushes and trees all around were lit up with multi-coloured lights and groups of people were walking over the grass, talking and laughing.

'Here comes the Morris dancers,' someone shouted. 'Move back a bit everybody.'

All the guests formed a circle round the garden and the Morris dancers in red costumes and bells began to hop and skip, linking arms and singing and shouting.

There was a burst of applause at the end. Abbie peeped into a bush in a different direction and saw someone walking quickly across the grass, carrying a glass of punch. A girl was hanging onto his arm. It was Diane.

'Oh, John,' she said. 'I didn't mean it. I didn't mean it really.'

'You don't know what you mean half the time, Diane.'

'Oh don't be so cruel, John. And don't look at me as

though you're analysing me all the time.'

'It's all your imagination, Diane. You have no control over your imagination.'

Abbie winced in sympathy for Diane who stood miserably holding an anchovy cocktail stick in one hand and a sherry glass in the other. Someone shone a light on Diane and Abbie noted with approval the emerald and coffee outfit she was wearing. In the half-light Diane stood stock-still and stared in Abbie's direction.

'That's Abbie,' she said. 'It's a woman at my office, standing just over there by the cherry tree.'

'You're hallucinating, Diane,' chuckled John. 'You shouldn't drink so much.'

Abbie moved back behind the tree.

'I could swear I saw Abbie,' Diane insisted.

Abbie ran quickly over the grass across the road, down a side-street and paused for breath behind a row of lorries. Her good intentions had come to nothing. Diane was not enjoying the party even with the new outfit. Abbie's secret watching of the spectacle had convinced John that Diane was hallucinating and Abbie had been too cowardly to reveal herself to them and say hello.

The walk had been a crazy idea – the idea of a little child, petulantly trying to break free of the bonds of normality. She heard footsteps coming from the other end of the road. A man and a woman appeared, carrying some packages. They were both middle-aged and very fat.

Abbie suddenly burst into tears.

'What's the matter dear? Are you ill?' said the

woman.

'No, just tired. I'm too tired to walk all the way back to Westminster and I haven't any money.'

The couple glanced at each other in amazement and then gesticulated to Abbie at the lorry. She climbed in the back.

'You ought to be careful, wandering about round here at this time of night. You ought to know better, a girl of your age. How old are you?'

'Nineteen.'

'Seems very peculiar to me. You haven't been taking drugs, have you?' The woman clambered into the back of the lorry and got out some black knitting.

'No, I've had a row with my boyfriend.'

The woman pursed her lips and raised an eyebrow. 'Oh, I see.'

She leaned to the front of the vehicle.

'She's had a row with her boyfriend, Gerry.'

He turned round. 'Sounds very strange to me, but anyway I'm going through Westminster so I'll drop you there.'

The lorry chugged through the wide streets, away from the river on a shortcut to Westminster. Abbie looked through the windows. The sky was almost black and there were no stars. She felt that the sky was mocking her and turned away.

Then she remembered a summer's day in her childhood, when lying on her back sunbathing on the garden lawn with her brother, the sun had gradually disappeared behind a cloud.

'You can work out how long it's going to take for the

sun to come out just by looking at how long it took it to reach that cloud,' he said.

She had thought about this for a few seconds. 'But doesn't the sun just go in sometimes?'

He had laughed. 'Come on, Abbie. Where do you think it goes?'

Now, looking up again, at the black sky, she realised that the disappearance of the stars was only a blindness, a concealment.

As if reconciled, she smiled to herself and leaned against the side of the lorry, and let herself be tugged to and fro with the rhythm of the vehicle.

23   The Seder

'WHAT ARE you laughing at Jeremy?'
'Robert. He looks so funny. If you chopped off his head and turned it upside down, he'd look like George Bernard Shaw.'

'Are you mocking my hair?' said Robert. 'I should inform you that I have just had it cut.'

Jeremy squealed. 'You can't have done.'

Joan looked across the table at her brother Robert, who was ruffling his fingers through the centre of his hair. She looked down at her cousin Jeremy, who was sitting on her left. He was small for an eleven-year-old and because he was so much younger than his cousins, they tended to treat him like a little boy.

As the youngest child in the room it had been Jeremy's role for the past six years, since the age of five, to recite the *Mah Nishtanah*, asking the elders of the family the four ancient Passover questions.

By now Jeremy had the *Mah Nishtanah* down pat and would recite the Hebrew quickly and confidently. After the questions had been asked, the story of how Moses, with God's help, had led the Jews out of captivity in Egypt to Israel, the Promised Land, as retold on every Passover night since the Exodus, would follow in the order laid down in the Hagaddah.

Over the five millennia history of the Jews many hundreds of thousands of different editions of the Haggadah had been printed and tonight as always the variations between them were still the subject of heated discussion and argument among the family elders.

Joan remembered celebrating the Passover meal – *Pesach seder* – almost every year for the past twenty years and always the same people were present. Next to Robert sat Andrew, Jeremy's brother, tall and pale and always trying to counteract his own natural solemnity by telling jokes, just as Robert tried to compensate for his own natural levity by adopting a serious tone.

Robert passed a dish of fried fish to Andrew.

'Thank you humbly, sir,' said Andrew, passing it across to the table to Joan.

'What's the matter, Joan? You're very quiet,' said Robert.

Joan placed a short slab of fish on her plate and cut into the layers of white flesh.

'Nothing,' she replied.

'She's busy looking after Jeremy,' said Andrew, 'and what a tough job that is.'

Jeremy put his hand over his mouth, which was crammed full of potato salad, and shook with laughter.

'I think he's drunk too much,' said Robert. 'He's taken the service so seriously that he's actually drunk all four glasses of wine already. No wonder he's tipsy.'

Jeremy hiccupped. He hunched over his plate of salad and strands of his blond hair flopped into the coleslaw and tomato, and Joan found herself giggling uncontrollably like a nine-year-old.

Jeremy looked up at her, pushing his hair out of his eyes. 'If you giggle, I'll tell Danny that you coughed all through the seder.'

There was a sudden silence. Andrew looked embarrassed and the aunts and uncles whispered to each other. Joan put down her knife and fork.

'Danny's ... not alive any more, Jeremy.'

Jeremy blinked, and suddenly changed from a little boy to an eleven-year-old.

'Why ... How?'

'He was killed in Israel in a border incident.'

Jeremy slowly chewed some lettuce while he tried to absorb this shocking news.

'I'm sorry ... I didn't know,' he said. 'Were you going to marry him?'

'I don't know,' replied Joan.

'Are you still going to teach in Israel?' asked Andrew.

'I don't know.'

Her mother passed round the Haggadahs, the Pesach service books to each of the assembled family, and the seder service resumed.

Aunt Gerda started reading a prayer in Hebrew but then stopped abruptly.

'What's happened to Dora?' she said. 'She was supposed to be coming tonight, wasn't she?'

'I'd forgotten about her,' said Jeremy's mother Alice. 'I thought she was going to Edinburgh for the week.'

'No, she was definitely coming here,' Robert said. 'She's probably got on the wrong train. She'll be hours.'

Joan visualised Dora clutching her bags and cases and rushing down a platform to catch a train that would take her in completely the opposite direction to where she wanted to go.

'Poor Dora,' said Gerda. 'I can just imagine it.'

Joan looked at Gerda. She looked almost the same as she had done two years ago. She was still petite and elegant, smiling and coquettish even though she was in her sixties and within the family group. She retained her role as the youngest sister.

Yet as Gerda read, Joan realised that her voice had changed. It was still lilting, but was now the voice of an old lady. Perhaps this was because of the occasional whistle from her false teeth, or the slight croak as she lowered her voice.

As Joan listened to the Haggadah account of the exodus of the Israelites out of Egypt and their liberation from bondage and slavery, she wondered how long Judaism would last. Would it survive in future centuries, as it had done in the past. As she looked round the table at the heads bowed over their Haggadahs, she felt a sudden lurching of the heart. Perhaps Judaism was no longer relevant. Perhaps Christianity was nearer to the truth.

The voices around her muttered the words of the Hebrew prayer. Most of her family had devoted their lives to upholding the Jewish way of life. Suppose it was no longer true. What if Jesus had been the Messiah?

She looked at Uncle Sydney: his bald head gleamed beneath the lamplight. He had put all his energy into Jewish and Zionist causes. He was an indefatigable worker. As she looked at him, he leaned across to Aunt Gerda and pointed out a mistake in his Haggadah to her.

Joan looked away embarrassed, as though she had been intruding upon his thoughts. Even if the two religions were still relevant, one of them must have more relevance than the other, and she did not know which. She would never know, for she was not a scholar and over the centuries scholars had argued interminably about the meaning, origin and historical accuracy of the various manuscripts.

Danny had been killed in Israel two months ago, fighting for the Israeli cause for which he had given his life and she desperately wanted to know how true that cause was.

'This is a load of rubbish,' Robert whispered across the table, his face contorted into a sneer. Joan looked at the edges of his mouth, which turned down in parallel lines. Perhaps Robert was right. Perhaps religion was a myth. As they stood up, lifting their glasses of wine, Joan saw clearly how all the great religions or their could all be equally right or wrong.

The wine sparkled dark red, like clotting blood. She took three sips: Judaism, Christianity, Islam; and then three more sips: Hinduism, Buddhism, Atheism. The wine bubbled as she lifted her glass to her mouth.

Sammy, her father, got up and walked over to the dining-room door. 'This is where we open the door for Elijah,' he said and everyone smiled: this ceremony always amused them.

Sammy went back to his seat and started to mutter his prayers again, when there was a knock at the front door.

'It must be Dora!' Gerda exclaimed. 'How lovely.

I'm dying to see her again.'

Sammy got up again and left the room to answer the door. They could hear shouting and a scuffle and the next moment the dining-room door opened. They all looked up, terrified, to see a thin, haggard-looking man in his forties with a long beard; he was holding a carrier bag in one hand and a newspaper in the other. He sat down in an armchair by the fire, leaning his elbows on its chunky arms.

'God, he smells!' whispered Robert.

'If he cut off his beard and put it on top of his head he'd look just like Robert,' said Jeremy, but nobody laughed.

Sammy had turned pale with anger and fear. 'Would you please leave our home at once,' he demanded. 'We're in the middle of a religious service.'

He pulled the stranger by the arm, but he clung rigidly to the sides of the armchair.

'Sure, sure, I know when I'm not wanted,' he muttered under his breath in an Irish accent, 'but I'm so bloody hungry.'

'Oh dear,' said Alice, 'we can't really send him away. I mean, we must give him something to eat.'

'But he's so smelly,' said Robert.

Alice ignored him and heaped some food on a plate and standing as far away from the stranger as possible, passed it over to him with a knife and fork.

'There you are,' she said.

He began to eat, muttering indistinguishable words between mouthfuls of food.

Gerda smiled benevolently at him. 'Isn't it funny that

he should come in just as we got to the Elijah bit. It's the first time it's every happened in my life.'

The stranger looked up. 'Elijah, you say? The prophet indeed. I'm a man of God. I've been in touch with the spirits above, I can tell you.'

'Don't talk to him,' Sammy said quickly to Gerda. 'We don't know anything about him. He might be insane.'

'Shhh,' said Alice. 'We don't want to start any arguments.'

'Insane, you say?' said the stranger. 'Sure, I'm mad as a hatter.'

He stood up and Jean instinctively turned her head away in revulsion at the smell. He walked quickly over to the door and with his hand on the doorknob, he said, 'Blessings upon you all, my children,' as Sammy led him out of the room. They heard the door slam behind him.

There was a long silence.

'Oh dear, how peculiar that was,' said Alice. 'Do you think we should have asked him to stay for the rest of the seder?'

'Of course not,' said Gerda. 'It was very kind of you to give him the food. I mean, you can't just go walking into people's houses like that.'

'Perhaps he *was* Elijah,' said Robert and Jeremy squealed with laughter.

'Well, how do we know what Elijah looked like?' Robert persisted.

'It's very easy to mock us,' Alice said angrily.

'I'm not mocking. I'm telling the truth.'

'You've been mocking us all evening. I could see it in your face.'

'Now we don't want any quarrels,' interceded Gerda. 'Let's get back to the seder. You can read this bit, Andrew.'

Andrew read the Hebrew slowly and carefully, but towards the end of the passage he knocked over a glass of wine. The red stain spread rapidly across the table-cloth. He placed his serviette over the stain and continued reading.

Suddenly he stopped: there was another knock at the front door. This time Sammy was red with anger.

'I'm sick of this whole business!' he said.

They all sat frozen in trepidation as he went out again to the front door.

A middle-aged woman with two suitcases and a cheery smile was standing on the porch.

'Sammy!' shouted Aunt Dora. 'How wonderful to see you again!'

She bustled into the dining-room, her arms stretched wide open to hug everyone in turn.

'I had such a terrible journey. You'll never believe it, but I got on the wrong train!'

'Really?' said Gerda, feigning surprise.

'I know! Isn't it ridiculous? ... Darling!' she added to Jeremy, giving him a bear-hug.

She pulled off her black coat and flopped into the armchair by the fire. Her nose wrinkled up and for a brief moment there was a distasteful expression on her face, a look of surprise and apparent recognition; then she relaxed and smiled.

'I must tell you – all the time I was on the train I kept thinking of you all having such a wonderful time, while I was stuck in a second-class compartment, sitting opposite the most appalling-looking tramp. He smelt disgusting and I can't imagine how he could afford the fare.

'The trouble was, it was a single compartment and I couldn't get out because it was a non-stop train, so I was stuck there with this awful man, who smelt absolutely terrible. I can't really describe it.' She sniffed the air for a moment and started to wrinkle her nose again, but seemed to think better of it.

'What was really peculiar, though, was that he had this carrier bag and a newspaper, and as soon as the train got going he pulled a book out of the bag and, do you know, for an instant I could swear it was a Haggadah. But then I saw what the newspaper was and realised I must have been mistaken.

'What was it?' said Gerda.

'The *Catholic Herald.* Now why would an old tramp be carrying a Haggadah and a Catholic newspaper at the same time? And on Pesach too! Anyway it's lovely to be here and I can see you've had a wonderful seder.'

'Yes, it's been absolutely wonderful,' said Alice, handing her some matzah and a plate of fried fish.

24 The Message

ALL HER life Eileen Baxter obeyed her mother. Any disagreements between them made her feel uncomfortable and if she started to display any opposition, her mother's quick frown of anger would shake her into docility.

She could remember the summer holiday in Torquay when she was nine. She and her sister Jane had dug a deep hole in the sand and Eileen had hidden inside it, long after her mother had told them they were going back to the hotel for tea. Eventually she had been discovered giggling inside the trench, biting her knuckles half in fear, half in glee.

'Come out at once, Eileen,' her mother Sandra commanded. 'You're not a little girl any more, you know.'

It was true that Eileen was far from little: she towered well over the heads of all her contemporaries. Her height only served to make her docility all the more absurd.

Twenty years later, she was still living at home with her mother, and her common sense had taught her the value of taciturnity. One morning at breakfast Sandra handed her a long buff envelope. She scrutinised the postmark.

'It's from Dundee,' she said.

'I didn't know you had any friends in Dundee.'

'I haven't,' Eileen replied, and Sandra, surveying her daughter, turned away ashamed at herself. She should have known better: Eileen had so few friends at all at home in Sudbridge that the question had been absurd.

Eileen bent over her toast, spreading marmalade in neat streaks. She was now well over six foot tall; her short, fuzzy hair fell over her forehead onto her spectacles. Her profile was angular – a series of bony projections.

'Are you teaching all day today?' Sandra asked.

'Only in the morning.' Eileen tore open the envelope and read the letter.

'Something interesting?'

'Yes.' Eileen stood up and collected together the pile of exercise books on the dresser.

Sandra smoothed down her apron, plunged a dirty casserole dish into the washing bowl, picked up a teacloth and began drying the crockery on the draining board.

'What is it?'

'I've got an interview this afternoon for a new job. It's to teach children with special needs in Dundee.'

'In Dundee? But why on earth would you want to go up there? It's so far away. You don't know anyone there.'

Eileen took out her fountain pen and wrote something in the margin of her marking book.

'Good experience.'

'But you'll be so lonely. And it's so sudden.' She suddenly put down her teacloth and stared pityingly at her daughter. 'Is there some man involved?'

Years of docility had almost wiped away Eileen's sense of humour, but not quite.

'Of course not,' she laughed. 'They're setting up a new college for special needs kids out there. It's a new project. It's unique and there's nothing like it in London.'

Sandra put her hands on her hips. For once her desire to dominate was overcome by a terrible pity for her daughter.

'You'll be denying yourself all the fun in your life.'

Eileen slipped the remaining exercise books into her briefcase.

'What fun? What life? It's what I want to do.'

She returned home that evening to find her mother in bed. She lay beneath the pea-green bedspread and coughed thickly.

'I've got bronchitis,' Sandra croaked. 'It's very bad.'

For the next few days Eileen brought up Sandra's meals each day with forced kindness, their normal conversation replaced by an almost loud silence.

A week later Sandra was still in bed when Eileen received the letter confirming her new post. She handed it to her mother and felt a sense of guilt when she saw how tiny Sandra's head looked against the white pillows. Her hair, once dark brown but now turning grey and white, now seemed half invisible within the sheets and pillows.

Eileen went downstairs to the kitchen and realised

that she and her mother were bound together by a bond of pity. There was no love between them. It had been obliterated by years of enforced intimacy.

A month later, on a Saturday morning, she was ready to depart. She had gathered together her suitcases and went upstairs to say goodbye to her mother.

Sandra was still lying in bed, staring at the ceiling, her face devoid of expression.

'You'll be lonely,' she said.

Eileen sighed. Her mother's complete knowledge of her entire life-history made any attempt to deny this quite impossible.

'Goodbye, Mum. And do get up soon. You'll feel much better,' she ordered her with a wry smile and ran downstairs. As she opened the front door, she hesitated.

'Goodbye, Mum,' she shouted.

There was no reply.

The journey to Dundee did not tire her. It was a cold March day, but she was exhilarated by the white sky, visible through the windows of her compartment.

She reached the college grounds at ten o'clock in the evening. The sky hung over softly like black charcoal. Inside the common room a group of people were sitting around a coal fire. A stout man with a huge beard stood up and shook her hand.

'I'm Roger,' he said and introduced her briefly to the others.

She sat down in an armchair, patterned with green leaves against a beige background. The room was warm and old-fashioned and she fell into a doze by the fire and felt again the novelty of independence as though she had just broken out of a cave and was floating in the sea, free to drift in any direction.

The days passed quickly, crammed with lessons and games with the children. Each Friday she wrote a long letter home, but there was never any reply. She would ring her sister Jane every week to ensure that her mother was keeping well and every week the news was always the same: Sandra was in good health, but very quiet.

After each phone-call Eileen would sit on the carved brown chair by the telephone in the corridor with her head in her hands and brood for several minutes. But she would always be called out of her reflections and reminiscences by the children.

One of them became her special charge. Her name

was Teresa, Roger's daughter, a five-year-old Downs syndrome child, who walked unsteadily, only half-seeing behind her pebble glasses and understanding very little.

But Teresa knew her own hair was red, because it was the one remark everybody made to her when they first met her: it was a mass of ginger curls which shone like copper in the sunlight. Teresa would point to her hair and whisper '*red*'.

As the months passed, Teresa began to speak a little more. Eileen, who had spent years of taciturnity in her own home, would now spend all her ingenuity in persuading the children to talk properly.

One day the children were playing in the school hall. The boys were running around, skipping and jumping on and off the stage; the girls were jumping up and down in time to a nursery rhyme.

'The music's too loud,' said Eileen and turning down the volume of the record-player, she heard the phone ringing. She ran out to the corridor, brushing against pictures of crayoned patterns that hung on the corridor wall.

'Can I speak to Eileen?'

'Speaking.'

'It's Jane. Mum's very ill. You must come home.'

'What's wrong with her?'

'Bronchitis.'

Again? Eileen thought, sceptically and sighed. 'Is it genuine?'

'Of course it is. It always has been. Don't be so self-ish, Eileen. She needs someone to nurse her properly.'

Eileen kept an eye on the open door of the school hall. Teresa had tripped over and lay crying by a chair. Her spectacles had fallen off and a boy had stamped on them and crushed the glass.

'I must go, Jane,' Eileen said hastily. 'I can't come home.'

'But you must—'

Eileen put down the receiver. As she looked at the telephone she felt that Jane's voice was still talking inside the machine.

She edged away from it and ran back to the hall. Teresa was picking up pieces of glass and was about to put them in her mouth. Eileen snatched them away from her and carried her briskly to a chair just as Roger ran into the hall and took in the scene. He returned a minute later with a dustpan and brush.

As he swept, he said, 'I hope you'll stay with us for a long time, Eileen.'

'I will,' she replied.

She ran round the hall, playing with the children, but her smile was forced. She felt a terrible weight inside her, as though she had deliberately committed a crime, and as the thought occurred to her, she realised that this was in fact the case. The energy she devoted to the children was no sacrifice, but she could not commit herself to the school in the way Roger was hoping.

When she rang Jane the following Friday the call was terminated abruptly after her first few words. A terrible fear seized her. Perhaps her mother was truly ill. She had to tell Roger straight away. She found him in the kitchen, pouring out glasses of milk.

'I've got to go home, Roger. It's an emergency. It's my mother.'

'I see,' he said, looking concerned. 'I hope we'll see you back here soon.'

'Perhaps – I mean, I hope so.'

She went to her room to pack and did not leave anything behind: she knew that she would not be coming back. She felt frightened and gripped by a dreadful sense of shame.

She carried her cases to the corridor on the first floor, together with her typewriter and carton of crockery. One of the porters helped her to carry the luggage downstairs. He went back up for the last case.

'You've forgotten your radio, miss.' He carried it down and placed it in her hand.

'I don't think it's working any more, Bill.' She switched it on and they could hear a very faint signal.

'Here, turn it up, like this.' Bill fiddled with the knobs and suddenly a voice on the radio rang out clearly.

' ... don't forget to prune your laburnums,' came the familiar voice of the question-master.

'It's *Gardeners Question Time*,' said Bill. 'My favourite programme. Laburnums – now, that's interesting.'

'And our next question is from a Mrs Baxter of Sudbridge. Over to you, Mrs Baxter.'

Eileen's heart missed a beat. She seized the radio.

'I'd like to know,' came an even more familiar voice, 'what to do about my miniature cacti. I've watered them a little too much over the past few weeks and they're beginning to droop.'

'Ah, that's interesting,' said Bill.

Eileen's face was rigid as she tried to catch every word.

'Alan, what's your opinion?' said Franklin Engelmann.

Alan Gemmell spoke authoritatively for a few minutes. 'Of course,' he concluded, 'looking after your plants, whether they're cacti or orchids, requires a lot of time and patience, and of course be careful in future not to over-water them.'

'I've got plenty of time,' came Sandra Baxter's cheerful voice out of the radio. 'Thank you Professor Gemmell, goodbye.'

Eileen stood at the bottom of the stairs, gazing at the radio in amazement, and then a wave of relief swept over her face.

'That was my mother,' she said. 'I thought she was ill, but she can't be – she sounded perfectly normal and healthy!'

Bill grinned. 'Well, I suppose I'd better be taking all that stuff back up to your room again.'

Eileen hesitated. 'No, I think I'll go home.'

'You don't have to.'

Eileen smiled and for the first time for a long time, she looked quite cheerful.

'I think I ought to,' she said.

25   An Evening in Rome

A WAITER TIPTOED softly across the red carpet of the hotel lounge and placed a tray of coffee onto the table in the corner. There were mutters of appreciation from the group assembled there. The accordion player by the window stopped his music abruptly and Anna's ears were shocked by the silence. She glanced across at her parents and felt a stab of pity mingled with irritation. Her mother picked up the coffee-cup, her little finger awkwardly elevated, and smiled artificially across at Mrs Dobson.

'They do know how to make coffee here, don't they?'

'Indeed they do,' replied Mrs Dobson.

Her father passed the sugar-bowl respectfully across to Rev. Dobson.

'In your profession a visit to Rome must be a unique experience.'

'It is,' replied the clergyman.

There was a long silence.

'Anna's training to be a nurse, you know,' continued her mother in what seemed to be a complete *non sequitur.*

'Really?' replied Mrs Dobson.

Anna sighed. She abhorred her parents' attempts to force a friendship with this couple, who looked utterly exhausted after the day's sightseeing. Yet, combined with this disloyal contempt, she felt an admiration for their imperturbable sociability. They seemed totally oblivious to the Dobsons' unwillingness to communicate.

The accordion player started his melody again.

'He seems to be very fond of playing "The Isle of Capri",' remarked her father.

Anna stared bleakly at the chandeliers that glistened in pinpoints at regular intervals across the lounge ceiling. The air hung heavy with a static tension. She noticed two rubber plants on either side of a pillar in the centre of the room. Their leaves were large and stultified by the torpor of the Italian summer heat. She stared at her cappuccino on the coffee table in front of her, at the froth and bubbles, which lay in white heaps, like the clouds she had observed on their flight to Rome.

From the other end of the room, she could hear the soft lilt of conversation, punctuated by frequent laughs.

'*Prego, prego, prego,*' shouted a voice, and another waiter slipped out of the room with clinical alacrity.

The dazzle of the chandeliers made her blink and yawn, and looking up, she saw that the clergyman was yawning too. He gave her a brief, conspiratorial smile and slipped back into the exchange of platitudes that had taken place every evening for the past four days.

Roberto, the tour guide, walked past their table and smiled charmingly at her mother.

'Is everything satisfactory, Mrs Harvey?'

'Oh, indeed. But there's just one thing. We didn't have enough milk this morning.'

Anna wearily detached herself from the conversation. Through the windows the stars in the sky sparkled invitingly in the black night. Anna looked up to see Roberto departing into the corridor and felt a pang of envy. The four silent figures suddenly appeared remote, like characters in a still from a forgotten movie.

'Such a helpful guide, don't you think so, Mrs Dobson?'

'Oh yes, he certainly is,' she replied.

'I think I'll go and do my packing for tomorrow,' said Anna. 'I've got so many packages to get organised.'

She walked slowly across the carpet, relishing its resilience against her tread and slipped down the corridor, past her bedroom, round the corner, and through the back door of the hotel. She stooped to pass beneath the black steps of the fire-escape and ran down the side-street, that led to the main road.

The fluorescent lights of the shops were dazzling. She walked briskly past the shop-windows, eagerly drinking in all the objects that flashed past her: gloves, umbrellas, dolls, ornate fancy-dress costumes for children, bottles of sherry, striped sweaters, gigantic boxes of chocolates and rows of silky ties. Her speed increased until she stopped to catch her breath outside a corner café. She gasped as a hand tapped her on the arm. It was Roberto and he looked angry.

'What are you doing running about all alone at night? It is dangerous. How old are you?'

'Nineteen,' Anna replied, still unable to catch her breath. 'I was so bored,' she added.

His thin lips appeared sickly in the yellow-green light of the café.

'You are a very silly girl.'

'What are you doing?'

'I'm on my way to visit my sister.' He looked anxious and disinclined to talk.

'Can I come with you?' she asked.

He shook his head slowly. 'No, she's ill. Hurry up. I'll take you back to the hotel and then I must go and see her.' He put out his hand to stroke her hair. Anna winced. 'I feel so trapped in that hotel. Couldn't I come with you – please?'

'She's in hospital.'

'I'd like to see what an Italian hospital is like. I'm a student nurse, you see.'

Roberto nodded silently. 'I know. I know. It's always the same. Young people don't want to sit and talk to their parents. The younger generation today is – how do you say – up the creek.'

Anna laughed. 'It's only eight o'clock and they'll sit in the lounge talking until midnight. I feel like a walk. Rome is so different at night.

Roberto smiled. 'OK, OK, but I'm telling you this. There is no fun to see my sister. She is very ill. And soon—'

An arm clamped down between Roberto and Anna.

'Alfredo,' said Roberto. They hugged each other. 'Alfredo and I were at school together,' he told Anna, 'before I got mixed up in politics.'

'Politics? I thought you were a courier.'

'Sometimes a courier, sometimes a writer, sometimes a politician. I do everything.'

'He does everything,' said Alfredo. 'He thinks he

knows everything. He is very big-headed.'

Anna laughed. Alfredo shook her hand. 'You're Roberto's friend so you're my friend too. Come in and have some coffee. We talk about old times.'

Roberto was smiling. 'Alfredo is noisy, but very harmless.'

They went into the café and sat by the window. An overpowering smell of bad cheese filled the interior, but Anna soon grew accustomed to it and watched with amazement, as Roberto and Alfredo vied with each other in recounting their political manoeuvres.

'You have any opinions?' Alfredo asked Anna. 'Yes?'

'No, I have no opinions,' she replied.

'Good, I don't like people to have opinions unless they know something. In that case they can have opinions. Otherwise, it is all rubbish. You thing we are funny,' he added as Anna smiled. 'The Germans, they are very solemn and the English, they are very proud.'

'Generalisations,' said Anna.

'No, it is true. But we Italians are friendly people.' He put one arm around Anna and the other around Roberto.

Anna suddenly remembered the hospital visit. 'Roberto,' she began, 'we must go and see—'

'And another thing,' said Alfredo. 'We don't just talk. We act. We make the effort to put into action what we believe. To have ideals, that is the important thing.'

'Roberto, have you forgotten—'

'We will have some wine. I remember Roberto when he was eighteen – as old as you, I expect.'

'I'm nineteen.'

A tall man with a pockmarked face carrying an accordion walked in and shook hands with the two Italians.

'Alberto!' they exclaimed.

Anna stared at the spot that disfigured his upper lip and suddenly felt frightened.

'Roberto,' she said, 'aren't you going to—'

'Alberto is a musician,' Alfredo explained. 'He will play for us.' He whispered something to Roberto and they both laughed raucously.

As Alberto began playing his accordion, Anna squirmed uncomfortably and then pricked up her ears as she heard the sound of footsteps and loud voices shouting in the distance.

'They are having a manifestation,' said Roberto.

'A what?'

'A manifestation. You know, a demonstration … for the trade unions.' His voice grew solemn. He spoke rapidly to Alfredo and they both lost their jocularity and began to talk very earnestly with many gesticulations.

Alberto continued to play and as his elbows shifted to and fro with the accordion, he explained the layout of the main roads in Rome to Anna in great detail. She listened, fascinated by the intersections and junctions, which revealed themselves in her imagination like the branches of a grapevine. They sat there for a long while, sipping wine and talking.

'And now what shall I play?' asked Alberto.

In spite of herself Anna, who by now could barely keep her eyes open, said, 'Play "The Isle of Capri".'

As the accordion played in rhythmic surges of sound, like waves rolling against crushed glass, her head, her head began to nod from the alcohol, and she slumped back against the wall in a disagreeable doze.

She felt a curious detachment from the situation, sensing that some political incident had taken place and that Roberto and Alfredo were engaged in further plans. As she lay there in a semi-stupor, the heat and colours dissolved into nothingness as sleep overcame her.

Once during the evening, she woke up and glancing at Roberto, whose face was strained and serious as he talked to Alfredo, she remembered his sister. She tried to open her eyes properly and to lever herself upright, but was dragged down by lethargy.

'Roberto,' she gasped.

He looked up and smiled. 'Yes, we go home soon.'

He muttered something to Alfredo and they both laughed. Anna tried to see her watch but her left wrist would not turn round when she wanted it to. Annoyed by this waywardness, she sank back into her chair and relapsed again into a doze.

Some time later she was shaken awake by Alberto, who squeezed his accordion noisily in her ear and a wave of energy ran through her as they stepped out briskly onto the pavement. Alfredo sang a pop song, punctuated by remarks in English. The cars roared past them out of alignment, and the road seemed to be heaving with restless vehicles.

A breeze rustled through Anna's hair and she began to feel light-headed. The heaviness in the air had lifted and snatches of conversation drifted past her as they wove their way between other groups of pedestrians. They reached the front door of the hotel and as Anna climbed the flight of white steps, she looked down at the three men, who now seemed squat from her bird's eye view. She sneezed and Alfred mistaking the noise, replied 'Ciao' and grinned like a cheerful chimp.

She hurried up the corridor and as she approached the lounge, she slowed her pace and walked thoughtfully up to the table in the corner where the group were still sitting by the window, exactly as before. Mrs Dobson was now drinking a fizzy lemonade.

They sat there motionless and silent, and yet somehow unified. Anna almost felt that she was intruding upon them. She walked as slowly as possible, consciously placing one foot down after the other, like a Victorian schoolchild about to undergo the discipline of having supper with its parents for the first time. She sat down next to her mother.

'Are you all packed now, dear?'

'Yes.'

'The journey to Sorrento tomorrow will be lovely – except for Roberto, of course.'

'Roberto? Why, what about Roberto?'

Her mother looked serious. 'It's very sad. He had a heart attack in the kitchen tonight. Just after he'd been talking to us. They found him lying on the kitchen floor. It's a terrible thing.'

Anna stared at her in bewilderment. 'But Roberto ... I mean, his sister—'

'Apparently he hasn't got any family. His only sister

died a year ago today. Isn't it a terrible thing ... Ah, here's the coffee.' She handed Anna her cappuccino. She stared at it on the table in front of her, at the froth and bubbles, which lay in white heaps, like the clouds she had observed on their flight to Rome.

Her mother lifted her little finger daintily. 'I do think they make coffee beautifully here, don't you?'

26 The Disappointed Woman

MURIEL HAD been parted from her husband for eight years and since then had struggled rather ineffectively at bringing up her three children. When I first met her, she was working as a typist in a very easy-going office, but even in this comparatively harmless atmosphere she managed to create violent quarrels with her colleagues. When she was in a good mood she was very amusing and would describe her household in precise, vivid and uninhibited detail.

'I know exactly what will happen when I get home,' she said one day. 'When I get in the kitchen I'll say to Linda – that's my sixteen-year-old – "Why haven't you made the dinner?" and she'll say to me, "Nag, nag, nag, nag, nag, nag," and then I'll say to her, "Go and take off your shoes."'

'But Muriel, why don't you punish them, when they don't obey you?' I asked her.

'Well, it isn't so easy in my position. Mind you, it was very different when my husband was at home. I'll never forget the time I got home late and discovered he hadn't been to work – he'd just been lazing around all day – but do you know what? He'd put on a little apron and made us a little supper – a veggie shepherd's pie, I think he called it. Well, of course at the time I was so cross about him not going to work that I just threw it straight on the floor…'

'I don't blame you.'

'I know but I suppose really I shouldn't have done that, especially as he immediately walked out of the house and went straight to the pub.'

'Muriel, how awful for you!'

'Yes, I suppose it was – especially as I may have saved his life that night.'

'How?'

'Well, he had a nut allergy and would probably have died of anaphylactic shock if he'd eaten it. He'd probably started drinking already, because he used ground nuts instead of soya mince.'

'You must have been relieved.'

'No, I was quite disappointed.'

'Why?'

'Well, if I had realised there were nuts in it, I obviously wouldn't have chucked it on the floor. But it was all right, because I scooped it all up and put it in the fridge. And then the next evening I served it up for his supper. Luckily he'd drunk so much the night before he'd completely forgotten that he'd made it himself with those nuts.'

'Muriel! He could have died!'

'Yes, that's just what he did, that very night.'

'But I thought you said you'd been parted from him—'

'Yes, I was. "Till death us do part," as we said when we got married.'

'So you were pleased that he died?'

'No, disappointed.'

'Why?'

'Because now I have to make the dinner. Can't trust Linda to do it ...'

27 A Square Peg

'HAVE YOU heard the latest bit of gossip?' said Lisa, packing her raincoat into a red holdall and walking to the office door.

'No?' replied Cheryl curiously.

'Rebecca has walked out on us. She left at lunchtime and there was a note on the table to say that she's decided to go and live in Hampshire. Isn't it hilarious?'

Lisa walked quickly out of the office giggling and Cheryl stared out of the windows at the office blocks opposite. It was easy for Lisa to laugh at Rebecca. It was easy for anyone to laugh at Rebecca. She was so patently efficient. Her position in the firm as Chief Administrative Officer laid her open to jealousy and admiration.

Lisa always used to call her The Robot, because she obeyed Mr Gillespie's instructions down to the last detail, and she was discovered to have made one mistake. She compensated for this by redoubled energy the following day. Cheryl was always in awe of her, because she was one of the few people who literally tried their hardest in every way.

The image of Rebecca as an efficient automaton had been bandied around the office ever since Rebecca had been promoted to her present high rank and Cheryl had always joined in the jokes at Rebecca's expense until one Friday afternoon, when Cheryl had been sent on an errand to the bank to collect some small change.

She was walking through the park when she noticed Rebecca sitting knitting on a deckchair behind a clump of rose-bushes and a fountain. The sight was so incongruous to Cheryl, who was accustomed to seeing Rebecca behind a typewriter and a row of record cabinets, that she had to slip a hand over her mouth to hide a smile.

The garment Rebecca was knitting was a long shapeless patchwork scarf of reds, oranges, mauves and yellows. The mingling of these colours caused an unpleasant tingling at the back of her neck, and she turned away quickly to the rose bushes to regain her sense of balance.

She pretended not to notice Rebecca and carried on walking to the bank. On her way back, she passed the same spot in the park and this time Rebecca was lying back in her deckchair fast asleep.

Cheryl was alarmed by this time. Rebecca never took afternoons off, especially Fridays, and her face looked white in the afternoon sunlight. She tapped her on the shoulder and Rebecca's eyelids flickered open and she looked up angrily.

'I'm sorry, but I was worried in case you were ill or anything.'

'Of course I'm not ill.' Rebecca snapped. 'Everybody seems to label me as some kind of calculating machine. Nobody even allows me to sunbathe in peace.'

'I'm terribly sorry.' Cheryl felt embarrassed and frightened that she might lose her job for being impolite.

'I'm sick of Mr Gillespie. I'm tired of Dr Hammond

and I couldn't care less about the computerisation changes. All I want to do is to sit and knit in the sun and I'm not even allowed to do that.'

Cheryl looked at Rebecca. Her eyes were glinting angrily behind her steel-rimmed spectacles and hair was a fuzzy mass of yellow-grey curls.

'If I'd had my way, I'd never have this wretched firm,' Rebecca continued, raising her voice. 'I always wanted to work on a farm. Or I might have made a very good nurse or a teacher. At least you get some thanks in those professions for your dedication.'

28   The Dentist

HE WAS RATHER small and thin, with streaks of sandy hair and strange, nervous grey eyes. He stood there, hesitating and restless, wondering how long his present colourless yet secure existence was going to continue. The room seemed nakedly chilly today, in contrast with the dancing, effervescent sunlight outside. The walls gleamed white and surgical, and the damp air carried on its back queer, cruel odours.

'Come in,' he yawned as the next patient tapped on the door. A girl entered breezily, curly blonde, brisk and jolly. She settled herself comfortably in the angular dentist's chair.

'That's right,' he said. His voice was unpleasantly soft. 'And what are you doing at the moment?' he asked.

'I'm still studying.'

'Oh yes, of course. It's Archaeology you're reading, isn't it, Miss Davies?'

'No,' she smiled. 'Chemistry.'

'Oh.' He seemed disappointed. 'Now why did I think you were reading Archaeology…?'

'I don't know.'

'But you do want to go to Greece soon, don't you, Miss Davies?' He seemed insistent.

'Not really.'

She has begun to gaze through the window at the

sparkling green and red garden beyond. The pear tree was beckoning her, the peonies were huge to the point of absurdity. Their big, flat, red faces nodded at her cheerfully. The sky was shining like a gigantic pale-blue china dinner plate. Down by the pond at the bottom of the garden a trellis seemed to be collapsing from the weight of the thick, clinging roses.

The girl sat absorbed in the bright, chequered shadows thrown by the delicate, lacy trees onto the lawn. The cold, grey dentist's room had been erased from her awareness by the golden lake of greenery in front of her.

She could dimly hear the dentist muttering to himself in the distance, 'She's not going to Greece, not going to Greece.' But even as she thought, *What an odd little man,* she was mentally smelling the velvet dust of the wine-coloured roses, and while the dentist gloomily assembled his instruments, she imagined the delight of lying on the rich green grass and being drenched in flickering sunlight.

29   Waiting for the Bus

THAT NIGHT Jean and I hurried home from the office, because the air was inky with rain and wind. We just missed the bus, and since we had a ten-minute wait, Jean embarked on the history of her short-lived romance with David, the boy who sat next to her at work.

He was a tall, bespectacled boy, remarkable only for his lack of individuality. I had noticed that he worked very hard at his irksomely mechanical office-job, and displayed a subdued, low-profile but dogged attachment to Jean.

'Did I tell you about that ghastly time I went skating with him?'

'No, what happened?' I asked.

'Oh Lord, it was *dread*ful! Well, I just happened to mention one day that I was going skating, and he positively invited himself to join me, which was jolly awkward for me, because I was already going with a friend. Anyway, I said vaguely something about seeing him outside at 7.30 if he decided to come and – would you believe it – there he was, absolutely on time. Well of course, I crept in with my friend, hoping he wouldn't notice me—'

'And did he?' I interrupted.

'Oh no. He was much too busy eating a hot dog, And honestly, if there's one thing I can't bear, it's seeing people eat in the middle of the street … I suppose it's snobbish of me, but I can't help it. It's just the way I've been brought up. Well, the poor thing stood outside waiting until nine o'clock. I felt so awful afterwards.'

'Did he eventually come in and skate?'

'Oh yes, that was the awful thing. You see, he was blue with cold and he'd never been skating before – and just imagine, he was dressed in his ordinary office clothes. Actually, I rather admired him for that: at least it showed that he wasn't trying to put on an act.'

'Wasn't he annoyed at all?'

'Oh, no. That's the dreadful thing about David. He's so submissive. I like a boy to have ideas of his own, and of course he's hopelessly uneducated.'

'Isn't he going to French classes every Wednesday?'

'Yes, I told him to go. That's why I can't bear him. He does everything I tell him to do. Anyway, to return to our skating outing, I introduced him to my friend Veronica. Heaven knows what she thought of him. You know the way he speaks. And I suppose he was jolly good on the ice really, considering. In fact, I admired the way he persisted, because we weren't exactly encouraging.'

'Did you go home together afterwards?'

'Well, we tried to make excuses, but he positively insisted. Of course, it was hopeless trying to make conversation at his level, if you see what I mean.

'So the next day at work, I let him realise that I disapproved of his behaviour, and he's been all right since then. In fact, at Christmas he gave me a record of "Blue River", which I thought was rather decent of him. Only, it was rather awkward, because I had got wrapped up in my bag the very same record for him. In fact we had a good laugh about it. Oh yes, he actually laughed. Well, it was Christmas time, you see.

'I suppose really I've been rather mean to him, but he is rather – you know – and my mother's brought me up to look down on that type.'

30   The Young Grandmother

I WAS RATHER surprised on the second day at my new job when Irene, the typist in front of me, an attractive, middle-aged woman, came up to me and whispered in my ear:

'How old would you say I was?'

She looked about fifty.

'Thirty-nine?' I hazarded.

She laughed triumphantly.

'Everybody says that! Actually I'm forty-seven!'

'No, really?' I was actually quite surprised.

'And do you know what?' she declared.

'No, what?'

'I'm a grandmother!'

This really was news, for she flirted with all the workers like a young girl.

'Yes, I've got four children and three grandchildren. It's impossible to believe, isn't it. Of course, none of them here know about it. You see I had to lie about my age to get this job. I said I was forty ... So you're the only one who knows the truth!'

I reflected on this. It could make me either a prophet or a blackmailer – or both.

In the event I simply became the accomplice in an innocent but delightful cover-up. Every day some incident would occur to make me aware of my superior knowledge. When Irene produced a small piece of white knitting, which she said was for a friend of hers. I alone knew that it was for her fourth grandchild-to-be.

I would have lunch with her and two others but when they both went on holiday, she was able to indulge in reminiscences of her wartime experiences of bringing up four children, for she had told the others that she only had one child.

'During the war I used to read a terrific amount. I'm extremely well-read, you know. And reading was my only solace in those days, apart from religion. I was deeply religious in those days...

'I always remember our curate saying to me, "Mrs Bassett, *you* have got a happy soul." And it's absolutely true, though I can't bear my husband...

'But I think I'm happy because I'm honest about things.'

31   The Unspoken Words

I T WAS four o'clock on a Sunday afternoon in Oxford. The bells of the clock in the college opposite began to chime and then echoed away, leaving a muzzy after-tone in the air.

Sheila looked around the room. It was long and narrow, shaped like a toothpaste-holder. Scarcely any light was able to enter. The dark furniture and red carpet flickered with the shadows of the afternoon. The gloom was broken only by the orange dazzle of a vase of Chinese lanterns in the corner. She passed round slices of ginger cake to the three other girls, who sat on the bed and on cushions, reading books and newspapers in silence.

Alison was crouched over a colour supplement. Her hair hung round her neck in a thin silky sheet. In the daylight it was almost white, but in the reflected light of the flowers it gleamed a pale orange. Deirdre sat in an armchair next to her, nibbling her cake thoughtfully and flicking over the pages of the collected works of Chaucer. Behind her, stretched out full length on the bed, lay Janice fast asleep, her head buried in a cushion and her arms neatly folded across her chest.

Sheila tiptoed to the sideboard to fetch some more milk.

'We're not very lively today,' said Deirdre with a yawn. She picked up a notebook and began to scribble comments in the margin.

There was a knock on the door. Janice sat up, rubbed

her eyes and swung her legs to the side of the bed. She patted the elfin strands of her hair into place, so that they framed her face like a bonnet.

'Come in,' said Sheila. The door opened. 'Good heavens, it's Aunt Clara. What a lovely surprise.'

She rushed to the door and escorted her aunt inside. She went back to close the door but it pressed against her and a man entered.

'I'm so sorry, I didn't see you in the dark,' she added.

'This is my friend, Paul,' said Clara, pulling off her gloves and heaving herself into the armchair by the fire, Paul sat down beside her.

'You're just in time for tea,' said Sheila.

Her aunt lifted up a plump arm ruefully. 'You mustn't let me eat too much cake darling. I'm trying to lose weight, but it's useless, isn't it, Paul?'

He smiled. Sheila looked at him curiously. He sat gazing at the fire, his hands folded over his knees and his eyes half shut, beneath thick brows. They were an odd shape. They almost met in the middle.

As if sensing that he was being watched, he looked up at her and said, 'Sheila. You're an energetic person, I see. Domesticated and happy. You'll be married next year and within a few years you'll have three children.'

Deirdre passed him a plate of biscuits.

He smiled at her. 'Thank you, my dear.' He took a biscuit and bit off the corner. 'And you are Mary Martha.'

Deirdre flushed as he said this and spread out her fingers. They were roughened from voluntary nursing at the local hospital.

Janice walked over to the bookshelf. Her movements were elegant, effortless. Her eyelids flickered for a moment as Paul turned to her.

'And you will be successful, my dear, in the academic world. And you will deserve it.'

Alison folded together the pages of her newspaper and approached him, looking him full in the face. 'And what about me?'

He stared at her in silence. Her face was white and very beautiful. His eyebrows were folded into one line and he turned away.

Clara smiled and clapped her hands together. 'You mustn't mind Paul,' she said. 'He comes out with the most peculiar remarks.' She turned to Sheila. 'Darling, I hope you've got enough warm woollies with you for the winter. It's so cold in this part of the world. I noticed it coming up on the train, but it seems even colder here.'

Sheila shivered. The room had suddenly turned very cold. She knelt by the electric bar heater and switched on an extra bar. The red light sizzled and the room began to grow warm. In the distance they could hear the sound of men laughing, and there was a sudden banging at the door.

It burst open and Pete walked in, beaming red from the cold. He bent down over Sheila's chair and kissed her on the cheek; then he warmed his hands in front of the fire.

'Peter, this is Aunt Clara. And this is Paul.'

Two hours later, when all the guests had left, Sheila

was piling the crockery into the sink.

'Aunt Clara's a dear, isn't she. And what did you think of Paul?'

'Odd bloke,' said Pete.

Sheila dug a teaspoon into the bottom of a cup, trying to scrape out some sugar that had crystallised at its base.

'Bother – this sugar's like ice.' She scooped with the spoon again and the cup snapped in two.

'Careful there,' said Pete. He picked up the broken fragments of china and threw them into the rubbish-bin. 'You haven't ticked off your calendar today. It's the 8th of November, not the 7th.'

'Oh no, I've just remembered. It's Aunt Clara's birthday today. I should have brought her a present. She must be fifty-five.'

'She doesn't look it.'

'I do wish I remembered.'

'Never mind. You can buy her something extra special for her sixtieth birthday.'

Sheila possessed a good memory for details, remnants of conversations and unimportant snippets of the past. Exactly five years later, when she and Pete were on their way to Clara's sixtieth birthday party, she reminded him of this conversation, but he had forgotten it completely.

'You women seem to hoard up memories of the past like old bottles of perfume.'

Sheila smiled at the image. Her dressing-table drawers were cluttered with tiny glass bottles.

'I know. I'm a mine of useless information.'

They arrived at the front door. It opened slowly. Sheila flinched as she recognised the dark face and the long eyebrow.

Clara pushed him out of the way. 'Hello, darling. I'm so glad you could come. So you managed to get a babysitter.'

'Yes. Two schoolgirls from next door. They're very good with children.'

They walked into the dining-room. A long trestle table had been set up in the centre with twenty or so guests seated around it.

'We seem to be late,' said Sheila. 'I'm so sorry.' She smiled and nodded at the bobbing heads bent over their grapefruits. Each head seemed to be set at a slightly different angle, with quick, fluttery movements of eating and talking.

Clara showed them to the end of the table. They sat down next to Paul, who had quietly slipped back into his place.

'Ah, you've met Paul, haven't you.'

'Yes, hello.'

He smiled quietly and continued to eat his grapefruit. The pointed end of his spoon cut quick slices in the flesh of the fruit.'

'I remember your delightful room at Oxford,' he said, 'and your charming friends.'

'Oh, yes,' said Clara. 'Sheila always used to have such nice companions.' She handed Sheila two dishes. 'What are they all doing now, dear?'

'Well, Deirdre's a nun in Ireland and Janice is lecturing in Wales.'

'Oh, how lovely. Well, isn't that nice to know. And what about that other little friend you had?'

'Alison.' Sheila put down her spoon. The atmosphere in the room suddenly seemed to chill. 'She ... it's difficult to tell you ... She was drowned in a yacht accident last year.'

'Oh.' Clara was clearly taken aback. 'How awful. I'm so sorry.' She looked sympathetically at Sheila and then began to rub her hands. 'We really ought to have coal fires these days. Electricity is no substitute.'

Sheila tried to swallow a piece of grapefruit, but it would not go down.

'Well, it's nice to see you both again,' said Paul. He smiled warmly, looking at Sheila. 'You will always lead a happy life, my dear. You have a happy nature.' He looked across at Pete. 'And your husband may not realise it, but he'll be happy too. Promotion at work, but without undue responsibility. And Clara. She spreads sunshine in a simple way, just by talking and entertaining. I can see her here in ten years' time.'

'Oh Paul, how nice of you. You do say some strange things. Now tell us a bit of gossip about yourself. I mean, you're a dark horse. I'm sure you've got lots of secrets about your own future hidden away.'

Paul looked at her. His eyes suddenly grew large and empty beneath the long eyebrow. The room felt very cold.

Sheila looked at Paul. Their eyes met. She shivered and turned away.

32   The Interview

'MISS PAYNE, will you come in please?'

The girl in the cream suit stood up self-consciously and disappeared out of the door.

Claire Russell looked round the reception room. There were only three other interviewees left. The tall woman in the corner looked listless, crossed her legs warily, and stared into the distance. In the other corner next to the window sat the two other candidates. They were both tiny and both also wearing cream suits. It seemed strange to Claire that such a large percentage of the women shortlisted for the post should also be wearing cream.

She glanced down at her beige raincoat. It had only recently been cleaned, but already looked marked. The two women sitting by the window were immaculately dressed and made up. The one on the left, who looked Chinese, suddenly tapped the shoulder of the fair-haired girl on the right.

'Sarah, isn't it?'

'Yes – aren't you Jean? My God, after all these years...'

Claire listened wearily to them as they caught up with each other's pasts. It seemed to her that the past was divided into portions. There was infancy and junior school, senior school and college and then work. And within each section was a kaleidoscope of images, people, fragments of the past.

Each fragment had a cord attached and these cords sank carelessly back into the realms of forgetfulness. But occasionally one could tug a cord and an image would spring up, as though trespassing between the segments of one's life.

Until recently these overlappings had always delighted Claire. They gave her a sense of the power of memory, which could overcome the limits of time and space, dissolve distances and bring two segments of different eras together.

But today the weight of the past hurt her, because of the letter she had written to Jan. She had tampered with the past and in revenge it had chosen to turn the tables on her.

She had first met Jan ten years previously on a barge holiday. It was a long narrow boat, drawn along by an old mare called Daphne, making a slow journey down the inland waterways of Wales.

There were twelve students on board the vessel – six women and six men. None of them had known each other before the trip. It had been organised by a company which advertised in the local newspaper and it had attracted an odd mixture of people.

The August heat had been intense and they had spent most of the holiday sunbathing on the roof of the barge. Each time Claire had swivelled herself up onto the roof, she had touched Jan by accident. He was always lying asleep near the edge.

Sleep seemed to be his natural state. He was an Austrian medical student, quiet and placid; Claire would spend time reading as she lay on her back and Jan would mutter odd comments to her as he awoke momentarily from his somnolent state.

She had been preoccupied during the holiday: having failed to obtain a place in a teacher's training college, she was halfway through her secretarial course. Feeling low and despondent, she had compensated by reading continuously and Jan, sensing this, had tried to drag her away from her books.

'Look at the scenery!' he would say. 'It's so beautiful.'

It was true. Claire could recall the glitter of the sun between the green leaves hanging over the banks of the canal, and their reflection in the water, so that it seemed as though the trees were growing within the water itself. In the distance, in front of the barge she caught a glimpse of Daphne's back, grey and drooping.

'Poor Daphne, she must get tired,' Jan used to say. 'We drive her too hard,' and as if to confirm this thought, halfway through the holiday Daphne drew to a halt by a clump of trees, and slowly began to chew the leaves.

Bob, the leader of the party, got out of the barge and ran along the towpath to try to move her on, but Daphne remained firmly entangled among the foliage. Bob and Jan disengaged Daphne's rope and attempted to pull the barge along by hand. To everyone's surprise, it did in fact move about ten yards, though Daphne was still ahead of the barge by the same distance again. Finally, the mare, looking up, satiated with leaves, walked demurely back to the front of the barge and allowed herself to be tethered to the rope again.

Jan climbed back on the roof and stretching out onto his back, fell into a deep sleep again.

One evening they were dancing on the roof in the twilight shadows. The canal water was dark green from the overhanging trees and the gypsy guitar and violin jazz of Django Reinhardt and Stéphane Grappelli's Hot Club de France from the portable record player drifted out into the damp evening air. Claire lay in the crook of Jan's arm near the edge of the roof.

'It's dangerous,' she said, looking down. 'We might fall off into the water.'

Jan laughed. 'It's good to take risks, and it is good to have friends. I'll tell you something: we are all here at this moment on this boat and we are all young. This moment will never come again. Maybe we'll meet again in ten years, maybe twenty … who knows.'

Claire snapped out of her reverie as the Personnel Department secretary put her heard round the reception room door.

'Miss Wilkins, would you come in please?'

The tall woman languidly walked over to the door

and followed her out.

The Chinese girl was laughing to her friend. 'Sarah, we must stay in touch ...'

Claire's heart thumped. If only she hadn't been so stupid as to write to Jan two weeks ago. After the holiday she had stayed with him in his apartment for several months, while she practised her shorthand.

The affair had been brief and not amounted to anything much. Most of the time he had been silent and preoccupied, and when he was not studying, he would lie stretched out on the rug in front of the fire with his eyes shut, listening to records. That was really the only way they had ever communicated, except when he made the odd, specious remark.

'You can always think of me as a friend.'

Claire had seized on these remarks eagerly, like a blackbird pecking at crumbs of cake. She counted them as an unexpected bonus, and would turn them over in her mind, sifting them and playing with them, examining them for any clues.

Several months later, Jan had returned home to Austria and Claire had completed her course. She found a steady job and the year had passed by quietly and uneventfully. Claire tended to consider herself as a nonentity, but a nonentity who came into contact with unusual people such as Jan.

Three years later she married the publicity manager in the company she worked for and they settled down to an orderly life in a semi-detached house near Beckenham.

Although still quiet, Claire had become energetic and

well organised. Small groups of people would drift in
and out of her house for coffee parties and dinner parties, and between the bustle of housework and entertaining, she always found time to read, to escape into
the world inside her mind where she felt she really belonged. And when two years ago her husband had been
killed in a car crash, she had borne it stoically and had
moved to a flat in London and taken on her old secretarial job again.

One day she was walking down a side-street in the
City. It was a cold, grey day: the sky was grey and the
pavements were grey and she stared down at her feet as
she walked along, having no wish to look up at the
bleak buildings on either side of the road.

A pair of grey trousers and dark brown brogues
wandered into the frame of the pavement screen of her
downward-pointing eyeline; there was something familiar about the look of them and the rhythm of their
movements. She looked up and it was Jan.

He smiled and said, 'Hello,' and as if he sensed that
she had been through a difficult time, he added unex-
pectedly, 'Are you still enjoying your work?'

'Yes,' she replied and for some reason did not wish
to carry on talking to him and walked on.

As the months passed, she would bump into him in
different parts of London from time to time and always
he would ask the same question:

'Are you happy in your work?'

Claire could never decide whether it was the question of a stranger or a friend, but as the months passed,
she realised that she *was* happy, and she was able to an-

swer his question in the affirmative.

One day she was standing in a bus queue talking to a typist from her office when someone prodded her gently on the shoulder.

'Hello, Claire, I recognised your voice.'

As usual it was Jan, but her bus arrived a moment later and yet again she did not wish to speak to him. After that day, she did not see him for a year and sometimes she wondered to herself why it was that she could not bring herself to talk to him. It was perverse, when he often recognised her and always spoke to her in a tone of intimacy, as if they were either still together or had only recently been separated.

One Sunday, when she was alone in her flat, she looked at the calendar on her wall, which as usual was crammed with engagements for the week ahead – several meetings, a dance, a sherry party, a visit to her sister-in-law and two dinner parties. They were all a typical part of her highly organised lifestyle nowadays and she no longer had any time left to read, to escape into the inner world where she felt she really belonged.

Were these people her friends? In a way they were and with them she could talk at great length, but was it real conversation? It seemed to her that only with Jan had she really been able to communicate, yet since they broke up she had always curtailed the possibility of conversation with him. Why? Perhaps he really was a friend, just as he had been all those years ago on the roof of the barge.

She sat down at the kitchen table and wrote a letter inviting him round for coffee. He had told her last year the name of the hospital – St Bartholomew's – where he was working as a senior house officer. As she sealed the envelope and addressed it, she felt that she was doing a foolhardy deed: after all, it had really only just been a casual fling. By writing to him like this, was she turning it into something more significant?

No longer would they be able to meet by accident in the street, knowing that the connection between them was buried in the past. If she sent the letter, whatever happened, and they were then to meet, they would be tied together by the present. Yet she was now somehow committed to the act of writing to him and ten minutes later the letter had been posted.

In the weeks that followed she felt an increasing sense of despondency as the days passed and there was still no reply from him. Every time the postman walked away from the front door of the flat, having left a pile of letters for her, she imagined it was Jan walking away indifferently, without saying hello. Six months passed and still there was no reply from Jan.

She looked up as the Personnel Department secretary opened the door.

'Mrs Russell, would you come in please – and so sorry to keep you waiting all this time.'

As Claire stepped across the pale blue carpet, it seemed to burn into her feet. Jan had not replied and she would never see him again. She had broken a secret rule governing the relationship between the past and present.

She entered the room and sat down in the chair facing a large desk, behind which sat the Personnel Manager.

He stood up and shook her by the hand. 'I'm sorry we've wasted your time, Mrs Russell, especially as you've had to wait forty minutes. However, I'm happy to tell you that you've got the job.'

She gasped. 'I've got the job?'

'Yes, we'd more or less decided it last week on the strength of your first interview, but after seeing your references and an example of your work and also after further consideration of the other candidates, we feel that you're suitably qualified for this post. My congratulations.'

He held out his hand to her again. 'We'll be sending you full details of your duties.'

She shook his hand and left the office. As she reached the bus stop, she recognised the man at the end of the queue. It was Jan.

'Hello, Claire.'

He spoke to her in a relaxed, even tone, as though she had never curtailed any of their conversations, or stonewalled his friendly solicitations when they had met in the street.

'Jan … Did you get my letter?' she asked nervously.

'Letter? What letter? No, I don't think so … Where did you send it to? I may not have told you but I'm no longer a senior house officer at Barts. I'm now a specialist registrar at Guy's. I'm working all hours, but I'm enjoying it. How about you? Are you happy in your work?'

Claire smiled. 'Yes, I've just got a new job. I think I'm going to be happy.'

'That's really great,' he said. 'You must come round

for coffee some time. I'll never forget that barge holiday … But that's all in the past. It's about time we caught up with each other in the present.'

She grinned. 'Yes, we should. I'd love to.'

226

33 The Tutorial

ON SUNDAY afternoon Sonya gave her friend Veronica an English tutorial to help her with her A-levels. Although nearly two years younger than Sonya, Veronica used to be her landlady and Sonya had lived in her Bloomsbury flat for four years.

The tutorial turned out to be a strange experience. She had known Veronica for exactly five years and during that time they had never really discussed anything seriously, or even sensibly. Instead they had always joked about everything, but since it was impossible to joke about *Paradise Lost*, they were forced to spend the two hours of the tutorial in total seriousness. She found this very difficult, and she also found an analysis of the poetry quite painful. It was so abstract yet naked in its ideas.

There was no real conflict in their discussion, since they were both religious. They were reading the first two Books of *Paradise Lost*, which were concerned with the fall of Satan and his plan to visit Earth. In a way these books were dealing with the most basic issues of life: the origin and nature of evil and its determination not to be subdued.

The kitchen was cold and damp, and Veronica's cat kept climbing up on Sonya's knee and digging its claws into her. Every time she threw the cat onto the floor with a thud, it jumped back up again.

It was exciting to discuss the first Book, and strange

to be exploring the landscape of Hell in Veronica's small kitchen where she had spent four years eating and laughing. It was also frightening. Suddenly the fridge and cooker no longer seemed to be real. They were simply contraptions of the twentieth century. The reality was the slow-moving shapes of the poem.

Sonya had made notes on record cards. Her handwriting was small and the ink was slightly smudged. After the first hour the dampness of the kitchen seemed to seep into her bones. She started to get cramps and was feeling bored. She suddenly had a sense of emptiness. The weight of Milton's ideas was too heavy for her.

As Veronica began to yawn, Sonya tried to liven up the lesson by relating *Paradise Lose* to Milton's life. They started to laugh and Sonya realised that it was very difficult to concentrate for more than an hour on poetry of that quality and intensity.

Whereas she had felt at one with Milton a few moments before, she now felt alienated from him. The pages of printed poetry dazzled her eyes. They were just words and bore no relation to the kitchen, the cat, the cooker or the fridge. They were the insane imaginings of a solemn, ancient poet.

And then an interest began to return. The imagery was vivid and they discussed the symbolism of light and darkness in relation to good and evil and to Milton's own blindness. Suddenly the poem became hugely significant: for several years ago they had both worked as readers at an organisation for the blind.

The poem was no longer an artificial set of words. It

was more real than the kitchen and the carpet. Sonya realised that the leaping cat would be dead within the next few years, that the flat would possibly be pulled down along with the many other mansion flats in Bloomsbury, but that the poem would go on existing over the centuries.

If Veronica and Sonya were to meet in forty years' time, they would both be changed. Perhaps they would both be grandmothers. Perhaps their beliefs would be different, but if they were to pick up Milton's *Paradise Lost* it would remain exactly the same – but would their interpretation of it be exactly the same?

The colours of the kitchen seemed ersatz and temporary. The patterned carpet had been dyed blue, but unsuccessfully. Blotches of deep blue alternated with large areas of watered-down pale blue. A raincoat lay thrown over one of the chairs and the draining-board was stacked with greasy crockery. The lace net curtains and the blue velvet curtains were greyed with time and dirt and one of Veronica's two fridges was cluttered with books of music and office files. They joked about this, nicknaming the second fridge 'Architecture' after Goethe's famous dictum: 'Music is liquid architecture; architecture is frozen music'.

In fact the kitchen was dingy and untidy; yet at the same time cosy and familiar. It was protective and oddly civilised, as though it bore no relation to the outside world, partly because of its lack of order within a world that was so disciplined and organised.

Even so, Sonya felt she had outgrown it and she wondered whether it was possible that her assumption that the atmosphere of the flat was deliberately Bohemian was merely her interpretation of it at the time. Maybe her imagination had now grown older.

And of course it was quite possible that in the years to come her interpretation of Milton would also mature and change, and that she would likewise think differently about her old friend.

34 A Break in Time

T IS half past three. The tea-break is over. The tea-lady carries away the cups. They clink, white and china, clear, unbroken white. I want to go on looking at them, drinking tea, thinking of nothing, but I am drawn back to the pile of bibliographies on the square table in the middle of my office.

Each book is heavy and old. The pages are soft and torn, crumbling at the edges. The print is tiny and faded. I open the volume L–R and check the details of three periodicals. The print is minute and shaped like an elm-tree. Letters and words flutter down the page, black on white, brown on white, grey on white, grey on yellow, a grey fuzz.

I shut the book and look out of the window. Office blocks, square and solid, unthinking office blocks, buildings that do not divide into thoughts and details, concrete that has no feelings, but simply exists.

The books do not simply exist. They vibrate with accumulated ideas, phrases and language. I look down once more at the L–R volume. Its navy covers are faded. The leather has been scratched and defaced by a bored predecessor, trying to stamp out its vibrant assertiveness with a sharp pen.

The pages are buzzing. Their edges are furred. Row upon row of tiny letters with notes scribbled in the margin. The navy letters written by the human hand, are a relief, a respite from the mechanical automatism of the printed word. The computer-like accuracy that has formulated this bibliography precludes imagination and whimsicality. Each page is blank on one side for amended entries.

Why shouldn't I scribble in a silly thought, a doggerel verse, or an insult, to break the monotony of the Reviews, the Proceedings and the Papers? Don't people exist as well as the printed word?

As I glance at the page, a billion sheets of printed paper float down before my eyes, edited, typed and printed, floating out of the printing presses from the past to the present; an iron eighteenth-century contraption in the basement of an Italian office; an underground newssheet put together in the dormitory of a French *lycée*. No feelings have come through. They have been filtered away by the heat of intellectual precision, leaving the printed word.

I glance down at the page again. It is no longer hostile. I see behind the volume numbers benign faces, a dark, bearded Spanish politician, a blond Scandinavian academic. The bibliography is not anti-human. It is the distillation of reason. Between the lines of conference proceedings and the papers of learned societies lie the remnants of a thousand human lives, employed in different spheres.

The Society of Antiquaries: a small bald head with frameless spectacles peeps out. The Institute of Electronic Engineers: square black spectacles and a cleft chin. The Philosophical Transactions of the Royal Society: a large elderly faces with grey sideboards and an expression of benevolent calm.

Words pour out. They flutter round me like an army of birds, friendly and stimulating. I am no longer alone, drifting between empty tramlines, frightened of an oncoming train of intellect that will run me over and crush me into blood and pieces of torn flesh. The ideas caress my hair and flutter up and down my arms, each word singing and resounding.

I am no longer in London, in England. I am in France, Nigeria. Melbourne. There is no limit to the individual existence. The tea-lady clattering the china in the corner of the room thinks she is in London. She does not realise that she is in the presence of all places and all ages. If only I could convey to her the timelessness of the moment.

She walks past my desk and a cup drops to the floor. It breaks into two pieces and the handle is cracked in two. She picks up one half of the handle and holds it between two fingers.

'Look at this love. Have you ever seen anything like it? Broken in half. I've never seen that happen before.'

The three other girls look up from their work. Their faces are expressionless.

'Half a handle,' she repeats. 'Isn't that extraordinary.'

'Very odd,' says the Supervisor. 'Mind you, these floors are so slippery, I'm not surprised you tripped.'

'But I didn't trip over, love. That's the funny thing. It just fell right out of my hand. Isn't that peculiar.'

I look at the bibliographies. They stare back at me guiltily. Could it be that they have been vibrating, that the reason the cup jumped out of her hand was the pressures of many times and many places and the strange atmosphere in the air? I dismiss the idea as a fantasy, delirious and illogical.

'Never happened before,' she says.

The books are silent and still. The timelessness has gone. We are back in London, in the twentieth century.